PRAIS

MW01253438

"A future vision as dark and compelling as the spaces between the stars."

—Gareth L. Powell, author of *Future's Edge* and *Embers of War*

"*Disgraced Return of the Kap's Needle* is a space opera filled with secrets and revelations, hope and addiction, along with the grief and struggle of a mother trying to save her fractured family."

—Ai Jiang, Nebula and Bram Stoker Award-winning author of *Linghun*

"A tense and tightly-paced thriller of greed, resilience, and community action. Reva, a formally high-ranking officer aboard the *Kap's Needle,* on the return journey from a failed terraforming attempt, will face her darkest fears; on the other side of her own power. Come for the disaster and decay, and stay for the sliver of hope that Bernardo so skillfully holds out, if only we have the courage to overcome ourselves and take responsibility for our actions."

—Eliane Boey, author of *Club Contango*

"Treachery and grief simmer below the surface, threatening one woman's sanity and the future of her crew in this deeply personal space noir from rising star Renan Bernardo."

—Jendia Gammon, Nebula and BSFA Award finalist author of *Atacama* and *The Shadow Galaxy*

"Twisted schemes and shifting loyalties abound in *Disgraced Return of The Kap's Needle*, and as with its morally gray characters, much more lies beneath the surface. Bernardo's timely tale is an affecting and thought-provoking science fictional allegory about the current state of humanity itself, and how dire straits lead us to extremes of both cruelty and compassion."

—Victor Manibo, author of *The Sleepless* and
Escape Velocity

DISGRACED RETURN OF THE KAP'S NEEDLE

CONTENT WARNING

This book includes mentions of drug addiction, suicide, and violence. Reader discretion is advised.

Edited by Rob Carroll
Book Design and Layout by Rob Carroll
Cover Art by Olly Jeavons
Cover Design by Rob Carroll

Library of Congress Control Number: 2025937515

ISBN 978-1-958598-74-0 (paperback)
ISBN 978-1-958598-87-0 (eBook)

darkmatter-ink.com

DISGRACED RETURN OF THE KAP'S NEEDLE

RENAN BERNARDO

DARK
MATTER
INK

*This book is for Mariza Bernardo, Taís Sanchez,
Jana Bianchi, and Julie.*

CONTENTS

KAPTEYN D, 2155 A.D.

Days before mission failure.

CHAPTER 01

ALERT: Keep your spacesuit on at all times when conducting research outside the ship. Breathable air does not mean safe air.

SURVEY-18734.LOG: With a viable atmosphere composition and stable climate, the planet exhibits con-ditions favorable for agriculture, scientific research, and long-term habitation.

HAHAHA. BULLSHIT.

Survey-18734 was how the AI probes had described Kapteyn d in their in-depth analysis. Hexabytes of surveillance logs and libraries filled with countless pages of auto-reports all promised the Kapteyn d expedition team a great future on the new planet.

All the data was wrong. The destination that ninety thousand people spent ten years to reach aboard the generation ship *Kap's Needle* proved instead to be a hostile ecology with no prospect for long-term human survival—in other words, a fucking cesspool.

First Officer Hannah Torres waited next to a solar-powered rover parked at the edge of the Purple

Forest, or whatever silly, unoriginal name the scientists had given to the millions of acres of dense, alien flora populated mostly by purple-leaved trees and giant, spiral-shaped mushrooms.

A team of five had gone into the forest to collect samples of potentially edible native plants for cultivation in their new settlement's greenhouses. The team consisted of two biologists, two armed Scouters tasked with protecting the biologists from any unforeseen danger, and one hanger-on to annoy them—Life Support Officer Reva Castro's fourteen-year-old daughter Alice. The duo of biologists was so overly excited that it was like they'd been sent to find chests of gold instead of whatever the forest had to offer.

Hannah checked her suit's biometrics on her wristpad, then wiped the helmet's visor to remove the fine particulates of regolith that saturated the hazy atmosphere. Kapteyn d was rich with breathable oxygen—just like the probes had reported—but the air near the Purple Forest was noxious and teeming with toxic spores that were constantly shed by the thousands of unstudied fungal species there. The spores caused people to vomit blood and hallucinate until death.

Hannah looked at her wristpad again. A younger version of herself stared back, a ten-year-old photo used as crew identification aboard the *Kap's Needle*. Her spiky blonde hair was free from grays at the time, and her skin free from wrinkles. If the woman in the picture could imagine where she would be in the future, she wouldn't have guessed anywhere close to this shitty planet.

A crack like lightning sounded from the forest.

"What the hell was that?" she mumbled. The ground beneath her feet rumbled steadily. She was about to radio in the disturbance when a stampede of large, elephant-like creatures burst from the tree line and thundered across the rocky plains that surrounded the Purple Forest. They were fleeing something.

One of her crew members sprinted from the woods in her direction.

Alice.

Hannah marched toward her as she approached. The girl panted and wheezed inside her fogged-up helmet.

"What the fuck just happened?" Hannah demanded. "What was that noise? And where's everyone else?"

"They're fighting!" Alice wailed. "Scouter Braga, I think he lost his mind! He shoved Dr. Wang to the ground! And then when Scouter Jones tried to stop him, Braga took a shot at him with his rifle!" Alice burst into tears.

Hannah grabbed Alice by the shoulders and shook the girl. "Stop! Look at me! Was Jones shot?"

Alice shook her head, her eyes brimming with tears. "I don't know. I don't think so. When I saw the rifle, I ran."

"Where are they now? Still back the way you came?"

Alice nodded.

"Fuck," Hannah said. She stared at the setting sun with disdain. She couldn't believe her terrible luck. "Keep your channel open in case I need to radio you for help."

Alice grabbed Hannah's wrist. "Where are you going?"

Hannah yanked her hand free. "To clean up your mess. Now get your ass back to the rover and stay there."

WHEN HANNAH ARRIVED at the scene of the fight, Scouter Braga was already down on the ground, unconscious, and Dr. Wang was attending to him. Braga's helmet was off, and Wang was injecting a fast-acting antifungal into the man's neck. After the injection was complete, he held two fingers against Braga's neck to measure the man's pulse with the sensors in his suit.

"What the fuck, Wang? You took his helmet off?" Hannah said. The skin on Braga's face had already become irritated by the unforgiving atmosphere. Boils had formed and started to ooze.

"I didn't," said Wang. "Braga took it off himself, right before he passed out. He was hallucinating bad and said he needed air."

Hannah looked over at Dr. Rezende, who was leaning against a tree, arms crossed firmly over her chest. Her lips were tightly pursed, and she was glaring at Hannah with steely, watchful eyes.

"Wait," said Hannah. "Where's Jones? I was told he might have been shot."

"I'm here," said Jones, returning from somewhere deeper in the woods. His helmet was also missing, and vomit ran down his chin and breastplate. Scouters were big men who wore bigger suits of armor made of neoprene and polyethylene, with sheets of reinforced Kevlar to provide extra protection against any hostile environment. His heavy metal boots crunched the wild underbrush with every step. He groaned, obviously suffering from some sort of severe abdominal discomfort.

Had everyone lost their fucking minds?

"Respirator was damaged when Braga shot me," said Scouter Jones. "It was either I ditch the helmet or suffocate. The armored plating did save my life, though. Took one right to the dome." Jones knocked a fist against his temple, then stumbled on some underbrush and caught himself against a tree.

"Have the hallucinations started?" Hannah asked.

"I think so, yeah."

"Give me your weapon. Knife, too. We can't have you armed if you're infected."

Jones handed over his rifle and hunting knife without protest.

"Why did Braga shoot at you, Jones?"

"I told you already. He was hallucinating," said Dr. Wang. His tone was angry, almost accusatory—accusatory, it seemed, of Hannah.

Dr. Rezende's eyes narrowed in disgust.

"Am I gonna die?" Jones asked the group. He was sweating profusely.

"I don't understand," said Hannah. "I thought Braga took his helmet off *after* the fight."

"He did," said Rezende. "But he was already sick by that time. Most likely, he'd been sick for days and just didn't know it."

Hannah shook her head. "How? What makes you think that?"

"You know how," said Wang.

"He told us everything on the way out here," said Rezende. She stood up straight, away from the tree. "He was stationed in the bio lab where you've been keeping your little secret. He told us about the spores you've been collecting behind the captain's back. Told us how he wanted to come clean but was afraid for his life. Said after meeting with you, he started to get sick. Found purple residue in the bottom of the coffee cup you gave him to drink."

Hannah scoffed. "This is preposterous," she said.

"Who's paying you to sell us out?" Wang asked. He rose to his feet. "What corpo wants the spores? I mean, why else would the first officer of the *Needle* consistently volunteer for these mundane biological expeditions? The only reason would be if you had something to gain."

"Guys," Jones groaned. "I don't feel so good." Then without warning, he started to vomit again. But this time, the bile was mixed with blood.

"Jesus!" Rezende exclaimed in horror.

"We have to get back to the rover," said Wang. "Our radios don't work in the forest, and we can't carry two hallucinating Scouters. But if we move fast enough, we can call for help." He marched past Hannah in the direction of the forest exit and the rover.

"Are you going to tell the captain?" Hannah asked, even though she already knew the answer. "About the lab?"

"What do you think?" said Wang, not bothering to turn around.

"Just checking," said Hannah. She raised Jones's rifle and shot Wang right through the back of his head. Rezende shrieked. The standard space helmet worn by the biology team was no match for the high-powered slug, and the visor on Wang's helmet exploded outward with exiting brain matter and blood. Hannah quickly turned the rifle on Rezende and fired two rounds into the woman's chest. While Rezende bled out, Hannah walked over to Braga and put a bullet in his brain. She then tossed the rifle next to Jones, who was now on his hands and knees, still vomiting the last remaining life within him. Hannah pushed him with her boot to see if he would react, but he just collapsed to the ground and started convulsing. He died moments later.

"GUNSHOTS!" ALICE SHOUTED as Hannah approached. "I heard gunshots! Is everyone all right?"

Hannah ran to Alice and started pushing the girl to the rover. "No, Alice, they're not. Wang and Rezende are dead. C'mon, we have to go."

"Dead? How?"

"Scouter Jones was hallucinating. He killed them. I barely escaped with my life." She grabbed the satellite phone from the rover and radioed back to the settlement, some five kilometers west. "I need an emergency evac unit at my location! We have a mass casualty event. I repeat: a mass casualty event. Sending the coordinates now." She climbed into the driver's seat and started the rover up. Alice jumped into the seat beside her.

"Give me your hand," Hannah said. "I need to remove your glove."

Alice's tear-filled eyes shimmered as she clutched her hands to her chest. "But why? It's not safe."

"We'll need to quarantine you if you're infected. And the first sign of infection usually appears in the fingernails. They darken."

"But...I didn't take my helmet off. I was never exposed."

"Yes, but you could have snagged your suit during the fight, or while running back."

"I—"

"I'm not asking, Alice. I'm ordering. If you want to play explorer, you have to obey the chain of command, no questions."

"O-okay." Alice gave her hand to Hannah.

A darkening of the fingernails *was* a real symptom of the infection, but neither Hannah nor anyone else knew if it was the first sign of infection, or if it was a symptom consistent across all cases. But Alice didn't know that. She just knew what Hannah told her.

Hannah unlatched the lock on Alice's glove and removed it. "Hold your fingers out so I can see them." Hannah took Alice's naked hand in her gloved hand, and with the top of the girl's hand facing up, gently rubbed her fingers on her palm and fingernails.

"Okay, you're good," she lied, then helped Alice put the glove back on and latch it. She forced a smile onto her face and patted the girl once on the shoulder in an awkward effort to soothe her. "Now, let's get you back to your mother."

KAP'S NEEDLE, 2162 A.D.

Seven years after mission failure on
Kapteyn d.

EARTH ETA: 1,351 days

CHAPTER 02

ALERT: Life Support System failure
detected. Oxygen levels dropping.

MR. BARCELOS HAD been sentenced: He would be
exiled to the old communications deck aboard the *Kap's
Needle*, where he'd live out the remainder of his days in
agony, slowly suffocating to death from a debilitating
lack of oxygen.

Not Reva's fault. She was just the messenger. She opened
the official arrest report on her wristpad and showed it
to Mr. Barcelos. He moved his face closer to the screen,
squinting to see better. Reva was losing patience. She yanked
him back to an upright position by the shirt collar and held
her wristpad up to his eyes. According to the report, Mr.
Barcelos was behind on payment for his allotted respiration
consumption, and he had not logged enough work hours
to reconcile the debt owed.

"Ma'am, I do believe I've worked for my air already,"
he said, slurring his words through a ridiculous grin. His
breath reeked of stale alcohol and the pungent scent of
processed cheese paste. "Just let me be, will you?"

Reva frowned.

Mr. Barcelos was just another tax evader addicted to
the narcotic known as Happiness. If he'd been sober in

this moment, he'd no doubt be begging her for mercy, demanding an inquiry into the ship's reporting, shouting about how his debt had been tabulated wrong. But as long as he was on the drug, the only fight he could muster was a weird grin.

Telling people they were wrong to breathe—*to live*—was the worst part of Reva's job, but lying to the innocent was a close second. Recent orders from the ship's captain had requested a quicker decrease in the number of O2 consumers aboard the *Kap's Needle*, so Reva got creative and started to convict passengers before their final bill had even come due. Mr. Barcelos was one of those cases. Reva found a strange comfort in his inability to know the difference.

"Mr. Barcelos, you haven't worked for…" she eyed her wristpad, "eleven days. You have not been paying for the air you breathe. In fact, your consumption has far exceeded your most recent allotment." A kinder, more compassionate Reva—the one she'd been during the *Kap's Needle*'s outbound journey—would have told Mr. Barcelos the truth, that he still had a week to make things right. But this was the return journey now. Reva was a different woman.

Mr. Barcelos burped, drool running from his lips and dripping on Reva's shoes. He swallowed, still flashing the dopey grin of Happiness. He would be dealing with a great deal of jaw pain when that thing wore off.

A team of biologists coming back from a card game on the mess deck saw Reva confronting Mr. Barcelos in the corridor and slowed their steps to watch the show as they passed. Reva threw a ferocious look at them, and they hurried on before they could catch any gossip.

"You know," Mr. Barcelos said, blinking repeatedly, "I don't owe you my obedience. I worked too damn hard for this ship, hauled too many crates back on that hellhole planet you people said would be habitable. I've earned my rest. This air I'm breathing is mine."

Reva shook her head, defeated. "If you won't come peacefully, I will be forced to call a Scouter. Is that really what you want?" She touched her wristpad's screen and opened the app to call them. It felt inappropriate to sic a Scouter on a slurring drunk like Mr. Barcelos, but she was in no position to argue with the captain's orders. Her finger hovered above the call button as she glanced one last time at the old man.

"Would you really do that?" he said with a twitching smile. "I have a son and—"

"So do I." She pressed the call button.

"What are you doing?!" Mr. Barcelos clutched Reva's arm, but she quickly spun out of his grip and pinned him to the wall with her knee. He wriggled in panic, but she just gripped his arms and shoved him back against the wall.

Behind them, boots pounded against the stainless steel floor like hammers. *Two pairs* of boots, by the sounds of it. The noise echoed throughout the corridor.

Two Scouters? Wasn't one enough?

Reva shoved Mr. Barcelos against the wall once more as the two armored guards approached, their faces hidden inside helmets with dark, tinted visors. Emblazoned on their chest plates was the sigil of the Kapteyn d expedition, once worn as a symbol of pride, but now a painful reminder of their hubris.

A loudspeaker in the lead soldier's helmet crackled to life. "Should I airlock this addict?" it asked. The sound was a distortion of the human voice.

"Of course not," Reva said. "Take him to O1—" She stopped and corrected herself. "To Orion-1." O1 was the nickname given to the old communications deck,

Orion-1, in order to scare debtors and antagonize the guilty. The deck was now a prison zone, starved of the necessary diatomic oxygen saturation to keep the entire incarcerated population alive. And since Orion-1 could be abbreviated to O1, which was also the chemical notation for highly reactive and incredibly lethal atomic oxygen, the nickname stuck. "Perhaps in six months, Mr. Barcelos can see his son again," she lied.

The two Scouters lifted Mr. Barcelos to his feet. "Hope you're healthy," one of them said to the man. "Your lungs are about to burn."

Mr. Barcelos groaned. He was sobering up against his will. The stress of the situation had probably triggered an early comedown response, and he was now suffering great psychological pain and seemed on the verge of passing out. With his frail arms wrapped around their armored shoulders, the Scouters led him away to a secure elevator that would take them many decks down to O1.

Reva had sent nine people to O1 so far this week, four of whom weren't warned about their rights and weren't given any chance to remedy their situation beforehand.

What am I becoming?

She cleared the name of Mr. Barcelos from her wristpad and marked his case as RESOLVED. As soon as she did so, a new court docket appeared on the device's screen. The name of the defendant paralyzed her for an instant: RÔMULO CASTRO, her son.

Not again.

She rubbed her eyes, but not to wipe away tears. Her sinuses were starting to act up again—a side effect of the ship's dry, recycled air—and she needed a decongestant and some rest. Now would be a good time to call it a day. Once she was safely inside her sleeping quarters, she could log on to the ship's Debtor Registry and erase her son's debt just like she'd done countless times before. If she were ever to be caught doing so, she'd be thrown into a brig, and her son would be without a corrupt mother to doctor his debts. But she had to take the risk. She couldn't bear to lose another child.

Her wristpad beeped, and Captain Horvat's face popped up on the screen before Reva could press CONFIRM. "Reva, I need to talk to you," he said. He scratched vigorously at his white goatee. Something troubled him. "In private."

"Okay. What about?"

"*In private*, Reva. Grand Conference Room. Thirty minutes." His face vanished from the screen.

CHAPTER 03

ALERT: Please repair the unresponsive CO2 scrubbers.

REVA SAT SLUMPED on the couch in her sleeping quarters, drinking generously from a bottle of whiskey while swiping through old pictures on her wristpad. The digital clock at the corner of the screen insisted on ticking forward. Twenty minutes until her meeting with Captain Horvat. She thought about cleaning up, concealing the circles beneath her eyes with makeup, becoming generally more presentable, but ultimately, she decided against it. In her mind, there was no longer a need to play pretend, and she was too comfortable in her silent misery to make the effort.

She swiped to the next picture. It was an old one of her son and daughter as little kids: Rômulo and his twin sister Alice. In the picture, the two held hands in front of a viewing window aboard the *Needle* and stared with wonder out at the billions of white lines that composed photospace. The siblings had always been astonished by the sight and often asked if they could touch the streaking lines or grab them as if they were threads. Reva's answer had always been a simple "no," but Alice never gave up. She insisted that one day she'd be able to reach those lines and spool them around her little fingers like delicate strings. And at times, Reva almost believed her.

The twins had been a miracle. Despite pregnancy being classified as a disqualifying condition for passage aboard the *Needle*, Rômulo and Alice had somehow managed to sneak themselves aboard as zygotes inside Reva's womb, the unexpected result of a one-night stand a few days prior to the ship's launch. Nine months later, they became the "Twins of the Kap's Needle," the only humans to ever be born aboard a generation ship, since the gestation pods were supposed to be activated only after the success of the mission.

After first learning of Reva's pregnancy from the ship's humbled physicians, Captain Horvat took immediately to reprimanding her, lecturing her profusely about every-thing from duty to contraceptives. Not that it was any of his business, but she *had* been using contraceptives at the time. Her babies had just beaten the odds. And she had never been happier.

Reva swiped to a picture of the twins as newborns sharing a cradle. They were so small at the time that they could fit together neatly in the crook of one arm. She swiped the photo app from the screen. Too many memories would lead to too much drinking, and too much drinking would lead to her missing her meeting with the captain. She needed to be sharp in case what troubled him had something to do with her.

She opened the ship's O2 report. Mr. Barcelos's future allotment had already been subtracted from the total supply, but there was still a lot of work to do, still more O2 to free up. She would need to prowl again soon, track down more criminal tax evaders and condemn them to death in the old deck. Maybe after enough poor souls had been purged, the quotas would end and Rômulo would be in the clear indefinitely, free to live as an unwashed stowaway until the ship finally returned to Earth. It wasn't likely to happen this way, but she would be foolish not to try.

She glared at the framed mid-century illustration hanging on her wall. It was an illustration of Kapteyn d, depicted as a smiling cartoon, its twin moons grinning in cheerful union. Written in playful calligraphy at the bottom of the image was the slogan: *Your new home awaits.*

Reva shrieked and hurled the half-finished bottle of whiskey at the sniggering face of Kapteyn d. It exploded in a spray of brown liquor and broken glass. The cartoon planet just continued to beam at her like a Happiness user too high to care.

EVEN THOUGH THE meeting was just the two of them, Captain Horvat had insisted on using the largest conference room aboard the ship—a room with seventy luxurious seats stationed around a grand, circular conference table at the center. Perhaps the room made the captain feel better about himself, made him feel as though the *Needle* was still humanity's single most important ship, and he its decorated captain. Or maybe he just wanted to get some use out of a room that had remained unoccupied for many years despite costing such a fortune. There was only one elevator to the large conference room. It was an all-glass enclosure with a panoramic view of outer space that grew ever more majestic with each passing moment. The design lacked practicality, but it was engineered this way in order to seduce influential politicians and wealthy venture capitalists and convince them to pour endless piles of money into the increasingly expensive expedition. *All in the name of science and the improvement of humankind,*

Reva remembered the claims at the time, never doubting for a minute that it was all in the name of profit. Science and the betterment of humanity had always been the secondary objectives.

But the extravagant elevator ride "up" that led to the conference room had worked. For when the rich and powerful suitors finally did arrive at the conference room, they were completely moved and eager to write a check.

Reva looked out at the void and the white lines of photospace that divided it. *No, Alice. You can't touch them.*

Captain Horvat was alone, facing the giant display screen on the far wall. Graphs and tables referenced and measured the ship's air consumption, its biospheres, and its life support systems. Reva knew the data pretty well. The ship's O2 levels were steadily decreasing. To put it bluntly, it meant more people would need to die in order for the ship to make it back to Earth with anyone still alive.

"So many problems," he said from over his shoulder, after sensing Reva's presence in the room. "We'll need to cull them all, eventually." He turned to her, his lips pressed tight. "The problems, I mean. Not the people."

"What's the difference?" Reva replied. "The people *are* the problem." She wanted a drink, *bad*. Needed it. She did keep a tiny bottle of whiskey hidden inside a pouch on her utility belt, but she wouldn't dare fetch it in front of the captain. He wouldn't care—would most likely ask for a sip—but Reva wanted to maintain some sense of decorum, at least until she knew the meaning of all this.

"Biosphere One and Three are dead," Horvat said. "And Biosphere Two is about to fail. It's inevitable that more people will need to be sent to O1 if any of the crew is to survive."

"We've already sent far more than originally intended."

Captain Horvat looked away. "I know…"

"It's a terrible way to go."

Captain Horvat scratched vigorously at his white goatee. "You think I don't know that? I've been to O1, Reva. I've seen firsthand the horrors we've unleashed. Save the lecture for someone else."

Thinking about the old communications deck meant thinking about death, and Reva hated thinking about death. She was never curious to see the abandoned deck or learn what happened there, not even disguised in a Scouter's armor like Captain Horvat had done once or twice. It was just the place she sent people to die. People shouldn't climb down into graves.

"What if we rotate passengers in and out of O1 rather than sending them there to die? We can even sell the idea as civic duty."

Horvat shook his head. "That will only lead to chaos. Passengers will return angrier and with a strong desire to dismantle the system that failed them. They'll have the motivation and the numbers to succeed." He scanned the graphs and tables on the screen. "If only we had more Refrimine."

"There are still a few cases onboard, mostly in the possession of technicians and doctors, but it's nothing we can't confiscate."

"Yes, but not in the quantities we need."

Refrimine was the main freezing agent in the cryopods, the chemical compound that made it safe to cryofreeze human bodies and keep them in suspended animation for long durations of time. After the first two biospheres inside the *Kap's Needle* collapsed, Captain Horvat had instituted a mandatory, emergency cryofreeze among the ninety thousand inhabitants of the *Needle* as a means to decrease O2 consumption as quickly as possible. The plan worked for ninety percent of the ship's population, but the

Refrimine supply ran out with nine thousand passengers still awake and in need of breathable O2.

Horvat opened his arms and gestured with both hands to the big display screen. "We're in a very difficult position. We have another four years until we reach Earth but barely a year's worth of air left to breathe." He closed his eyes and massaged his temples. His teeth clenched, and his jaw grew tense. "I admire your work," he said. "You're one of the best officers on deck…"

"But…?"

"But I'm relieving you of your duties as Life Support Officer, effective immediately."

"What? Why?" Her skin crawled. "Who's taking over?"

"I will be performing your assigned duties."

"I don't understand. Did I do something wrong?"

"No, it's nothing like that. This decision has nothing to do with your performance. I'm relieving all officers of their duties until I complete a ship-wide corruption sweep. There's a lot that's gone wrong on the *Needle* that needs to be fixed. We tried our best and failed. Now I need an honest assessment of our failings before time runs out."

"Am I being reassigned?"

"No, you're being put on temporary leave. I want you to take some time for yourself. Get some rest, spend some time with Rômulo. He needs you. We'll talk again soon, Reva. You're dismissed."

Reva knew she should follow orders and take her leave, but she couldn't.

"What does First Officer Torres think of all this?" The woman's name tasted rancid on her lips. Hannah Torres might have been exonerated by an emergency court in regard to Alice's death—and the deaths of Wang, Rezende, Braga, and Jones—but Reva would never be convinced. The things her daughter had said on her death bed… The physicians told her not to think much of it, that they were just hallucinatory ramblings, but Reva knew her daughter better than any doctor alive.

Still, invoking the dissent of the first officer in this moment could prove to be useful. Torres was so notorious for always voting against Horvat's decisions that Horvat called her "Ping Pong" because according to him, she hit back all his ideas.

"She's against the sweep…to no one's surprise," he said. "She says it's a waste of precious resources."

"But you're still going to go through with it."

"Of course. I'm the captain of this ship, not Torres."

The room seemed to close in around Reva. She imagined herself grabbing Horvat's shoulder, begging to be the one responsible for the sweep, pleading for him not to take away her only ability to protect Rômulo. Without officer credentials, she couldn't access the Debtor Registry and erase her son's ever-mounting debt.

But she was alone in the conference room, powerless, as if she'd been stripped bare. Perhaps the only person who could help her now was the woman she despised most.

CHAPTER 04

ALERT: Training facility is under maintenance. Due to low oxygen levels, please refrain from any physical exertion.

REVA RAN.

Sweat broke down her forehead, and she wiped it away with a towel. Exercise used to be the best way to reconcile her thoughts after Kapteyn d. The padding of her feet, the NeedleStream's distant hum on the terminal in front of her— she could almost pretend she was back on Earth. Perhaps if she closed her eyes, she could decelerate the treadmill to a stroll and head back to Brazil, to her beach house in Recife where she'd spent her vacations. She tried to picture the place, but the memories had become tarnished over time, faded. The city's warm, welcoming shoreline melted away, and she opened her eyes to the *Needle*'s cold, lifeless sterility.

My life is in photospace now.

She gestured over the machine's motion sensor, wordlessly commanding it to decelerate, and stepped off. She looked around at the near-empty deck. It used to be one of the ship's many public gyms before being incorporated into one of the many infamous mediwastes. This one, like all the others, had been decommissioned years ago after the Refrimine ran out and nine thousand bodies in need of respiration were left to fight over what little O2 remained. It was only logical for Horvat to close the gyms down. Exercise ramped up the body's metabolic functions, causing the lungs to consume far more oxygen than normal respiration. No sense in wasting oxygen on frivolous activities like jogging or weightlifting when everyone's lives were at stake.

But in a sense, it was merely a formality. Many passengers skirted the ban by exercising in the privacy of their sleeping quarters, free from Scouter surveillance teams. Artificial gravity wreaked havoc on the body, but a few push-ups and sit-ups each morning helped lessen endocrine stress. It was a therapy that most would never give up no matter how dire the ship's situation.

The *Needle*'s crew, however, didn't need to hide their opposition to the exercise ban. They had the mediwastes at their disposal—repurposed sections of the ship transformed into crew-only areas meant for "stress relief vital to the new mission." "Mediwaste" was the nickname given to these places as a way to mock the crew's selfish desires, a portmanteau of "meditate" and "waste." The mediwastes weren't meant for restful activities that lessened O2 consumption; they were exclusive clubs meant for drinking, gambling, dancing, playing, and having sex. They were for daydreaming about better days while running on a treadmill.

There weren't many people in the mediwaste gym today. Two female systems engineers spotted each other at the squat bar, and two male Scouters took turns on the bench press. A third Scouter, still in his full suit of armor but with helmet off and placed on the table in front of him, lounged in a plastic chair near the exit and took long drags from a cigarette.

Reva nodded to the Scouter, letting him know that she had finished her run. He nodded back and shouted at one of the two people at the bench press. "Salazar! Treadmill's open. Your thirty minutes starts now."

The Scouter scanned Reva's wristpad to clock her out and then scanned Salazar's wristpad to clock him in. She saw fifty taucoins being subtracted from Salazar's account. A small price to pay for the privilege. The Scouter took another drag of his cigarette and turned to blow it in Reva's face. "Something wrong, Officer Castro?"

Reva coughed from the smoke. "What's your problem?"

"No loitering. If you're done here, get moving." He nodded over at the exit.

That's when Reva realized she had been lost in her thoughts. The other Scouter was already on the treadmill, and she was still standing in the same spot.

It had been the taucoin transaction. It reminded her of Horvat's corruption sweep. Had he started a system-wide search already? It would only take a few hours for the system crawlers to discover the treason Reva and Officer Torres were guilty of in different ways. If discovered, she would almost certainly be thrown into O1. Rômulo, too. They'd both be dead within months.

There was only one way out. The idea had bounced around her head ever since her meeting with Horvat, but she had pushed it away every time until now. "Hannah is the way out," she whispered.

Her respect for Ping Pong ended the day Alice died on Kapteyn d, but Reva *could* be willing to push her animosity aside for the time being if it meant she could still save Rômulo. First Officer Torres wanted nothing more than to climb the ladder to captainship, and Reva knew that this obsession could be manipulated. She also knew what her daughter had whispered in her final moments, her eyes blankly staring at the walls. *My hands. She took my hands.*

Reva gave the Scouter a dirty look and took the exit he had nodded toward. Once back in the public corridor, someone grabbed her arm. Her first thought was that Mr. Barcelos had come back from O1 to settle the score with her, but when she turned, her eyes widened…

"Rômulo…?"

The twenty-one-year-old young man in front of her was gaunt and sickly, his cheeks sunken into his face. His jumpsuit was filthy and ragged, and bleeding sores festered on his forehead and lower chin.

"Oh my God," Reva whispered. "What happened to you?"

Rômulo smiled, and it lingered, and that was all it took for Reva to lunge forward and hug the boy tight. Rômulo returned the hug, but weakly. His arms were skinny, fragile, and Reva was afraid she'd break him if she wasn't careful. She felt awful for finding some relief in not having to look directly at his face while they hugged.

She withdrew from him. "You're sick."

He flashed his teeth, the smile turning into a grin, but his eyes were distant, flitting back and forth, as if looking for someone neither of them could see. *Happiness.*

Reva's eyes narrowed. "You're high."

"I'm fine."

"You're not!" She shook him by the shoulders, and when she let him go, he tumbled backwards. She grabbed his hand to prevent his fall. "Look at you. You can't even stand up straight. You're a mess."

Rômulo smiled and shrugged. "Like mother, like son, I guess."

Her heart stopped. "How dare you? Do you have any idea what I've been doing for you? The risks I've been taking. If it weren't for me, you'd already be dead, just another corpse on O1. If Horvat finds out, I'll be prosecuted."

"You don't have to do that," Rômulo said. "You should stop before you get caught." A tear streaked down his smiling face.

"Don't you care if you live or die?"

Rômulo motioned to the lonely corridor around them, the lights turned down low to conserve energy. Most of the rooms located along the corridor had been put on lockdown, their life support systems cut off, the people inside relocated or dead. "This isn't living, Mom."

Reva took her son's hands in hers. "Don't say that. Don't ever say that. You have to stay strong, keep pushing, if not for you, then for me. Just a few more years and we'll be back on Earth." She forced a weak smile. "You'll finally know your true home. You'll finally get to see our house in Recife. The one I've always told you about. You'll finally get to see Brazil—" She held Rômulo tight against her chest, no longer afraid of breaking him.

Rômulo sniffed, and his shoulders hitched as if he were about to cry. "What about Alice?"

"What about her?"

"She'll never see Brazil, so why should I?"

Reva closed her eyes. She was tired of her son acting as though he was the only one who grieved his sister. "What are you doing here?" Reva said. "It's obvious you didn't come to see me." She already knew the answer. She just wanted to hear him say it. There was only one reason why someone like Rômulo would wander into the mediwastes. He was looking for more Happiness.

"There's an extra bed in my quarters," she said, her eyes now flush with tears. "You can use the rest. Come back to me. Alice isn't here, but I am. Please, son. I need you."

But the feeling was not mutual. Rômulo lowered his head and left without a word.

CHAPTER 05

"TWENTY MILLION TAUCOINS in exchange for seven species of fungus. All samples must be alive and viable. Payment will be made discreetly in two equal transactions, half upon proof of retrieval and half upon delivery."

That was how Congressman Hepburn of the Western Earth-Moon Government had summarized his pitch to Hannah one month prior to the *Needle*'s departure. He told her he had a partner aboard the ship, one who represented a very powerful private enterprise, and who was very interested in acquiring the spore samples for medical and military research to be utilized outside of the ship's command. The private enterprise was never named, but Hepburn promised Hannah that they would have an outsized influence over the new settlements on Kapteyn d, and that it would serve her well to be in their good graces. Perhaps it could even lead to a captainship. They had that kind of power.

Hannah looked over the specs the congressman had provided her. "I don't get it. Why was none of this included in the drone reports? If we know the planet is toxic, then—"

"The planet isn't toxic, Officer Torres. Don't be dramatic. No one would be sending an expedition of this stature to a toxic planet. Only the spores are toxic. The reports are correct in their analysis of the atmosphere. The air there is identical in chemical composition to the air we breathe here on Earth."

"Yeah, but it says here that the fungus covers an estimated sixty percent of the planet's surface. This could be a mission-killer."

The congressman shrugged. "Perhaps. Every mission has its risks. But that's why this information is on a need-to-know basis. Too much money has already been invested into this project for it to be called off now."

"Does the captain know?"

"Horvat? No. And it has to stay that way. Understand?"

"Okay, so why me?" Hannah asked. "How do you know I won't go running to him right after we finish here?"

"Because I know ambition when I see it," Hepburn said. "I've read your file, Officer Torres. *ALL* your files. You have no more love for Horvat than I do. You don't just want money. You want so much more. And with your help, I can make that happen. Now, do we have a deal or not?"

"I don't know, I—"

"Prove *your* mother wrong, Hannah. Prove to your mother that you can be someone worthy."

HANNAH'S FACE ON Reva's wristpad made the life support officer want to shatter the screen into a million little pieces.

I'm doing this for Rômulo, she reminded herself.

CALLING...

"Reva…" Hannah's voice crackled on the wristpad's speakers as her face popped up. The transition from a young, professional head shot to the grainy video of a middle-aged woman in poor lighting was stark. It reminded Reva just how much time had passed since the day they departed Earth. Reva hadn't aged much better. "What the hell do you want?"

"You're fucked. You know that, right? If Horvat runs a corruption sweep and discovers what you've done—"

"You have some damn nerve!" Hannah said.

"I know about Congressman Hepburn."

Hannah's voice fell silent.

"I know about your lab, about the spores. I know that you purposefully infected Alice."

Hannah laughed nervously. "This again? I thought only dwellers believed in conspiracy theories."

"I have proof," said Reva. "But I'm willing to negotiate. See, I'm not innocent myself, and this corruption sweep is about to be a pain in both our asses."

"Meet me in the old casino," Hannah said. "Twenty minutes. And come alone. Fail to do so, and I'll ghost you." She hung up.

Something felt off about Hannah's eagerness to meet. The old casino was one of the first decks to be locked down following the *Needle*'s emergency departure from Kapteyn d, meaning it was without lights, oxygen, and surveillance. This made it the perfect place to plan mutiny, but also to commit murder. And Hannah was a killer.

Reva needed a backup plan, just in case. She opened the drawer on her bedside table, fetched a large knife, and holstered it in her utility belt.

THE ELEVATOR DINGED, and Reva stepped into the dark corridor that led to the casino entrance. She checked her suit's integrity on her wristpad: ALL SYSTEMS OPERATIONAL. She had one hour of oxygen before the tank on her back ran out. She clicked the helmet's forward-facing flashlight on.

Hannah's voice crackled in Reva's helmet. "Follow the main corridor and take the first left. I'm in the security room in the back. Door's open. You can't miss it."

The emergency lamps along the floor started to light up as Reva walked. They were on their own emergency circuit, and whoever shut down power to this section of the ship must have forgotten to also shut off the backup.

The glass double doors that had once welcomed guests to the casino had been shattered. Reva stepped through the door frames, careful not to snag her suit on any of the jagged remains as her boots crunched on the piles of broken glass on the floor. She walked slowly through rows of abandoned slot machines, their garish lights and sounds a distant memory, and past green-felt gaming tables with mahogany trim, the markings on the tables boasting everything from blackjack to craps. At one table, a broken roulette wheel sat lopsided on its axis, the roulette ball there forever stuck on twenty-four black.

She'd been in the casino a few times in the past. She recalled a game of blackjack where a group of dwellers loudly proclaimed the promises they were making to themselves to fulfill once they arrived on Kapteyn d. One would establish a village on the planet. Another would make a great discovery that could end hunger on Earth. A woman promised to explore the farthest reaches of the planet, documenting everything she saw. Reva had smiled at them, nodding at each promise they said out loud, not wanting to say anything. Because there was no promise she wanted to make at that point. She had everything. Her twins and the prospect of a good life on a new home.

She was nearing the security room in back when her foot struck something on the floor. She stumbled before steadying herself.

She looked back to see what tripped her, her flashlight moving eerily across the floor.

It was a circle of dead bodies. Twelve of them, to be exact. There were no signs of violence. In fact, the corpses held hands, which was how they must have died, to some degree at peace, or at least in communion. Their preserved faces inside their helmets made it difficult to decipher how long ago they had perished. Their eternal youth, free from age and decay, unsettled Reva in a way she couldn't describe. One of the faces belonged to a young woman, her eyes still partially open, and—

The face morphed into Alice's, and Reva stepped back. The eyes came to life, staring directly at her. The jaw slightly dislocated moved, exhaling stale breath onto the inside of the helmet's visor. "My hand!" it shrieked. "Why did she take my hand!"

Reva screamed again, but then a hand grabbed her shoulder from behind.

"Reva!" Hannah said. "Are you okay? What happened?" She spun Reva around and grabbed her by both shoulders to steady her.

"No," Reva muttered, feeling the tears warming her cheeks. "Not again. I can't live through this again."

The nauseating smell of wild, alien fungus and the sulfur-rich soil from which it grew assaulted her nostrils and made her instantly sick to her stomach. The smell of her daughter's death.

"Reva!" Hannah shouted. Her staticky voice echoed inside Reva's helmet. "Reva, snap out of it!"

And just like that, Alice's face was gone, replaced by the face of the dead woman.

"What the hell happened here?" Reva said in a hushed tone.

Hannah turned her helmet's flashlight to the circle of dead bodies, grimacing at the sight. "Fuck," she muttered. She knelt down and grabbed a discarded Refrimine ampoule from the floor beside one of the bodies. She held it up for Reva to see.

"I don't understand," Reva said. Her voice was failing. "Were they trying to cryofreeze themselves without a pod?"

Hannah tossed the ampoule to the center of the circle and stood up. "No one is that dumb. If I had to guess, this was some sort of suicide pact. The Refrimine was just how they chose to go out. Probably did it down here so the bodies wouldn't be discovered. C'mon, the security room is this way. We can talk more there."

While Hannah led the way, Reva toyed with her utility belt and the knife that was sheathed there. She could shank Hannah in the liver with one quick stab, then slit her throat while she was down. Then, Reva could throw her corpse atop the rest. No one would ever know what happened to her. If she was to believe in any superior design, perhaps this rendezvous in the casino was simply an opportunity granted to her so she could take revenge on the woman who murdered Alice.

"You'll keep that knife in your belt," Hannah said.

When they entered the casino security office, Hannah gestured for Reva to take a seat, but Reva chose instead to stand.

"Horvat is a dangerous captain," Hannah said, leaning against a table of powered-down security monitors. "He's not doing what's needed for this ship's survival. He's too old-school, too attached to the same old paradigms of power, thinking that if he keeps allowing dwellers to be sent to O1, things will come into balance. But you and I both know that's bullshit. The ship is depressed, Reva. Everyone onboard is falling deeper and deeper into despair. It's no wonder the use of Happiness has skyrocketed. People are tired. And the constant threat of slow execution by suffocation isn't helping. A depressed crew is an ineffective crew. Understand?"

Reva cleared her throat, thinking of what to say, but just nodded instead.

Hannah continued, "I know your work bothers you. It would bother me, too. Sending innocent people to O1, men and women that we celebrated with, toasted with, drank and smoked and gambled with right here in this very casino. Feels like treason, no?"

Reva had to give Hannah credit. She was excellent in the art of persuasion. Her thoughts floated back to the dwellers making promises to themselves during the blackjack game. Where were they now? Maybe suffocating their way back home.

"Not even treason. Feels like pure cruelty."

"And yet you're the one being forced to carry it out. Doesn't that make you angry?"

"I didn't come for counseling," Reva said. "We need to talk about the corruption sweep, about your deal with Congressman Hepburn. Your personal feelings about Horvat don't interest me."

Hannah studied Reva with great intensity. "Fair enough. So, what do you know about Hepburn, besides what idiots drunkenly whisper over drinks."

"I have record of your private emails with him," Reva lied. "They were part of the encrypted files Rezende sent my daughter before you killed her."

Hannah remained in silence. Reva's gamble had worked.

"Okay, so let's say I agree to help you in exchange for these files, what do you want in return? Why are *you* so afraid of the corruption sweep, Life Support Officer Castro?"

"I've been falsifying my son's O2 quotas so that he's not sentenced to O1. To balance the books, I've been prematurely sentencing dwellers who are in debt but not beyond reconciliation." Saying it out loud for the first time felt more like a confession to herself than to Hannah.

"Long story short, you send innocent men and women to die," said Hannah.

"Yes," said Reva, gulping the harsh truth.

"Okay," said Hannah. "Now that we understand each other, we can get back to my plan."

"Your plan?"

"Expose Captain Horvat before he can expose us."

"Expose him? For what? What the hell are you talking about?"

"You'll see. But first, can your wristpad still upload videos to NeedleStream?"

"I don't know. Can yours?"

"No. My permissions were revoked. Won't return until after the corruption sweep is complete."

"Then I'm in the same boat."

"Just check, will you?"

Reva checked her wristpad's connection to NeedleStream, expecting her access to be denied, but to her surprise, the connection was still active. "I don't get it. All my other permissions have been revoked. Why not this one?"

"Remember that documentary they filmed back in the early days of the ship? It was meant to document the lives aboard the *Kap's Needle*—"

"Yep. My children were featured, followed around by cameramen for weeks at a time."

"And as part of that feature, you were given special media access to NeedleStream, were you not? So that you could help document the twins' lives more intimately. Well, I had a hunch that *maybe* your media access was never revoked. Turns out I was right."

"And the captain doesn't have control over private permissions," Reva added, now starting to understand.

Hannah handed over a storage card inscribed with the NeedleStream's logo. "This card has some footage of Horvat that might interest you, might interest the entire ship. All I need is for you to upload it to the NeedleStream and set the broadcast to 'Public.' I'll take it from there."

"What's on the video?"

"You can find that out later. Right now, I need your commitment."

"And then what? Horvat is relieved of his duties, and you become acting captain? No, thank you. I'd rather be sent to O1."

"And Rômulo?"

"I…"

"Think about it, Reva. There would be no corruption sweep under my command. And whatever you're guilty of, I'd bury it. I'd exempt Rômulo from the O2 quotas, and you'd never have to lie for your son again. Never have to *kill* for him again."

The plan was tempting, but still, Reva was torn. She'd always admired Captain Horvat. He had guts. He was the one who managed to stretch three years of the mission's resources into five. He was the one who trusted that the ship's engineers, biologists, and chemists would devise solutions for the venomous soil and the air that carried the Purple Forest's spores. He was the one who willed a seedling to grow in a controlled environment outside the ship, even though it would die less than six hours later. And he was the one who put an end to the mission on Kapteyn d despite strict orders to the contrary. When demanded, he made the required sacrifices without complaint, even going so far as to cast his own career reputation into the fire so that he could bring the ship and all its people home. Reva would never have thought to betray him had he not mentioned the corruption sweep first.

"Where'd you even get this?" Reva asked, holding up the storage card.

"That's not important. What's important is what's on that card."

"And yet, you've just been holding onto it this whole time. Never thought to tell anyone."

"Let's just say I've been waiting for the right opportunity. And the right person to share it with. So, are you with me?"

"I'll think about it," Reva said.

"You have twelve hours to decide," said Hannah. "If the video on that data card isn't uploaded by midnight tonight and scheduled for broadcast tomorrow morning, I will order your arrest for high treason."

CHAPTER 06

ALERT: The number of psychother-
apists available for appointments
is now zero. For self-help, please
consult *The Kap's Needle Guide to
Well-Being and Mental Health*. It's
available for free on the ship's
library network.

ASTROGATOR THOMPSON HELD *Rômulo
in his arms and spun around in circles, causing
both he and the boy to laugh. "We're going to the
moooooooon!" he shouted, lifting Rômulo up into
the air as they spun.*

*"We're light years beyond that old rock," Reva
joked, rocking Alice in her lap.*

*"Right," Thompson said. "We're going to Kapteyn
deeeeeeee!"*

*Rômulo giggled as Thompson spun him around
some more.*

*"These are the Twins of the Kap's Needle," said a
NeedleStream documentarian to her camera. "And
today, we're teaching them how to identify stars."*

Reva turned her wristpad off and removed the storage
card. She tossed the card back into the desk drawer with

all the rest and wiped the tears from her face. There were dozens of storage cards in the drawer, most of them episodes of *The Twins of the Kap's Needle,* which comprised a large part of the broader documentary series produced for NeedleStream with the intention of building morale aboard the ship and ramping up excitement back home on Earth during the first years of the trip.

During her fruitless attempt to sleep following her secret meeting with Hannah, Reva had dreamt of Rômulo. He was calling the elevator, heading to the casino, but without a spacesuit and oxygen. Reva ran to warn him, but the corridors lengthened under her feet, and the elevator doors shut just before she reached him. But not before she caught a glimpse of the grin that lined her son's face. She woke up sweating and, not wanting to go back to sleep, spent the rest of the evening revisiting her past through storage cards.

There was only one card she had not yet viewed: the one Hannah had given to her. She eyed it suspiciously. What if it was a trap?

There was only one way to find out.

Reva grabbed the card from the desktop and inserted it into her wristpad. The screen went black. The PLAY option appeared at its center, and she touched it.

A video was loaded, scrambled at first but then clear, or at least as clear as the shaky camera would allow. The shaking stopped, and the face of a bearded man with hoop earrings appeared. The camera was recording him as he hid the device inside what appeared to be a potted plant. He took a seat at a table now perfectly centered within the camera's frame. A while later, another man entered the room and took a seat across from the bearded man.

The other man was Captain Horvat.

The recorded conversation between the two men was short, but what they spoke about was enough to end Horvat's career on Hannah's terms rather than his own.

"So, all I have to do is turn a blind eye?" Horvat asked.

The bearded man nodded. "Just keep us open and twenty-five percent of the take will be yours."

"Thirty percent," Horvat countered.

The bearded man grinned. "Fine. Thirty percent."

"What kind of pharmaceuticals are we talking about?" Horvat asked. "I don't want this operation of yours to damage my crew's integrity. Limit the sale to dwellers only."

The bearded man waved away Horvat's concerns. "I'm not about to push anything crazy. Just some expired psychotropics. Pills for depression, anxiety, cluster B. I even have some narcotics if the need arises."

"Narcotics? What, like drugs?"

"Opioids, mostly."

Horvat pondered this for an instant, scratching his goatee.

"People need pain relief, captain," the bearded man said.

"The ship's physicians—"

"The ship's physicians won't prescribe meds that have been damaged. And almost all the ship's meds have been damaged. I, on the other hand—"

"I get it," Horvat said flatly.

The bearded man leaned forward onto the table between them. "Listen, Captain, we just want what everyone trapped inside this tin can wants: a little bit of relief. Compensation, you might say, for the expedition's failure." He hesitated for a moment, then added, "A failure that happened on your watch."

"Thirty-five percent," Horvat said. "But no narcotics. Not yet at least."

The bearded man smiled and held out his hand to shake. "Deal."

Reva stopped the video right as Horvat completed the handshake. That recording must have been the bearded man's insurance policy in case Horvat decided to go back on their agreement.

So, the man who Reva admired was, in fact, just another asshole like the rest, herself included. It didn't surprise her. This floating hellhole required that you get your hands dirty. Those who tried to keep them clean didn't last long. Most were already dead. But what if Horvat's corruption sweep was just an excuse to wipe away his own illegal dealings? What if he had no intention of looking into the files of others? What if Reva was panicking over nothing?

In her estimation, she had two options. The first was to upload the video anonymously to NeedleStream. Horvat would be relieved of his duties and jailed without any knowledge of her involvement. Hannah would take over as captain, and all records of her past indiscretions would be erased. Rômulo would get a fresh start—*would have his chance of setting his foot on Earth*—and Reva would never have to worry about O1 again. The second option: inform the captain of Hannah's planned mutiny and reveal to him that they knew about his illegal dealings. Get Hannah thrown into the brig, where she'd no longer be a problem, and use the incriminating footage of Horvat to blackmail him—force him to erase her record and exempt Rômulo from all respiration quotas now and until they reached Earth.

It's one big chess board, she thought, *and I'm just a pawn.* Blackmailing the captain would be too risky, would be like a pawn trying to checkmate the king on its own, but following through with Hannah's plan and doing so anonymously was much more in line with her chess piece's capabilities. *Let the queen put the king in check.*

She looked down at her wristpad. The video of Captain Horvat was still paused on the screen. She tapped the SHARE button on the device and chose the option to upload the video to the NeedleStream. The video would broadcast in the morning.

CHAPTER 07

ALERT: Should you be summoned by a Scouter, kindly obey. Your compliance is crucial for maintaining law and order aboard the ship.

THUD! THUD!

Reva rustled in her bed. *Was someone trying to repair the settlement's domes again?*

Thud!

Reva was so tired. *Didn't they know Kapteyn d was a flop? Just stop and—*

Thud! Thud! Thud!

Reva opened her eyes.

"Life Support Officer Castro!" a machine-like voice shouted from the other side of the door. "Open up! If you do not comply within ten seconds, we will enter your quarters by force."

"Scouters," Reva murmured, and tapped the switch beside the bed to turn the lights on. She grabbed her wrist-pad from the bedside table. The screen showed nothing but black. She tapped the power button again and again, but it didn't work. *Shit. Horvat must have discovered their plan.*

She jumped out of bed and looked around the room for something to defend herself with. There was the knife, but striking a Scouter's armor with a blade was like a wasp trying to sting a rhino's hide.

The rock…

Back when they first arrived on Kapteyn d, Alice brought back a rock the size of a cantaloupe from the planet's surface and carved her initials into the stone's coarse exterior. After the girl died, Reva was forced to dispose of all her daughter's things—most of Alice's possessions had become contaminated by the spores—but Reva hid the rock in a secret compartment beneath her bed and kept it hidden all these years.

She unlocked the secret compartment, grabbed the rock, and positioned herself next to the cabin door. The rock wouldn't do much damage, but she hoped it could stun the Scouters enough to allow her to escape.

The sound of a sparking control panel on the other side of the wall meant the Scouters had successfully hot-wired the door's security and were getting ready to breech. A moment later, the door slid open, and the first of the Scouters marched inside, stun-weapon at the ready.

Before the Scouter could react, Reva jumped out from her hiding spot and smashed the rock into the side of his reinforced helmet. He recoiled, raising his arms, but when she attempted to flee past him, a second Scouter grabbed her wrist and closed its mechanically aided fingers around her slender bone.

Reva tried to push the man off her, but he didn't budge.

"Stand down, Officer Castro," said the first Scouter, whose helmet she had crushed. He had straightened back up, and his heavy metal boots were clanking about on the floor.

She spat at the Scouter's face hidden behind the tinted visor.

"Feeling feisty today, are we Reva?" said the one holding her. A mechanical laugh sounded in his speaker.

"Fuck you," Reva snapped.

"Enough of this. Let's go," the first Scouter commanded. He holstered his stun-weapon and grabbed Reva by her other wrist. "Captain's orders."

Together, the two Scouters dragged Reva through the ship's dim, maze-like corridors. She struggled to get free, but her efforts only managed to exhaust her.

Dwellers stood outside of their quarters, gaping at the confusion. One man gave her the finger, and another spat in front of her. She expected as much. Still, a few dwellers directed their anger to the Scouters instead of her. She wasn't loved around these parts, but now that she was an enemy to their enemy, she was afforded—or so it seemed—a small share of their sympathy regardless of her guilt.

A Happiness user pushed his way to the front of a crowd that had gathered at the mouth of a connecting corridor and jumped to get Reva's attention. "Mom!"

"Rômulo!" She turned her head to keep eyes on him while the Scouters dragged her past.

"Mom, I saw your picture on the NeedleStream," Rômulo called. He jogged after her.

"Back away, boy!" said the smashed-helmet Scouter. He shoved Rômulo hard in his bony chest, and the boy almost toppled backwards to the floor.

"Mom! It's Officer Torres! She's who ordered your arrest!"

Reva's heart skipped a beat. *Fuck.* This was starting to play out exactly like she had feared. Hannah was never serious about working together. *I should have taken the damn king,* she lamented.

The Scouters took a right at an ominously familiar intersection. Reva's heart sank. She was hoping to be brought in front of a court for questioning, but apparently that was not the plan. This was the route to O1. The Scouters weren't her jailers, they were her executioners.

Up ahead, a NeedleStream display was broadcasting a news alert to the corridor. On the screen, the ship's system relayed the alert. "Following the arrest of Captain Horvat for treason, First Officer Hannah Torres has assumed the role of captain. Her first order: the immediate arrest of Life Support Officer Reva Castro, who has been tried and found guilty of fraud, treason, and more than twenty counts of premeditated murder for her role in the wrongful deaths of all falsely convicted prisoners on Orion-1. If you have any information as to the whereabouts of Officer Castro, please contact ship administration or alert a local Scouter. DO NOT attempt to approach Officer Castro on your own. She is believed to be armed and dangerous."

"We've nabbed ourselves a real piece of shit right here," the smashed-helmet Scouter said to his partner—but really, he was saying it to Reva.

At the end of the corridor, a galvanized metal gate barred the elevator doors. The light here was a dull, reddish hue, barely enough to see by, but Reva could still read the faded sign on the wall beside the gate: COMMUNICATIONS DECK .

"We're here," said the smashed-helmet Scouter. He pressed a button on his suit, and a tiny compartment opened in his chest. He removed an ampoule. "I assume you know the procedure," he said to Reva.

She ignored him, but yes, she knew the procedure, even though she never witnessed it first-hand. The syringe contained sodium thiopental, used as an anesthetic. People tended to panic when they saw the bulky gates of O1, and panicked breathes were not ideal when entering a low-oxygen, CO_2-rich environment. The Scouters didn't care if the prisoners died eventually, but they didn't want them fainting before they could even be processed, or worse, going into fight-or-flight mode while sky-high on adrenaline.

After loading the ampoule into a syringe, the Scouter seized Reva's arm again, lifted her sleeve, and injected the fluid into her veins. Within moments, her vision blurred, and her eyelids grew heavy. Sounds that had once been clear were now muffled. Her legs, now weak, started to tremble, and before she knew it, the Scouters were the only things holding her up. The last thing she remembered was the horrible clanking sound of the gates as the Scouters forced them open.

CHAPTER 08

ALERT: Orion-1 is off-limits both to dwellers and crew. We appreciate your cooperation.

REVA WOKE UP sweating. Her heart nearly beat out of her chest.

Calm down. Remember your anxiety training. Control your breathing, relax your muscles.

"The tax woman woke up," a voice said.

"Does that mean we can beat her now?" said another.

"Spare your breath, you fool!"

Reva did her best to sit up and look around, but everything was a blur.

"How are you feeling?" said an old man with a long silver beard.

"Not good," Reva said bluntly. "Weak. My heart is racing."

The old man nodded. "What you're feeling are the effects of hypoxia and hypercapnia. But don't worry, you'll get used to it."

Crew members and dwellers alike encircled her, watching her every movement, their faces mixed with curiosity and contempt.

"Hope you die, bitch," said a woman, and a faceless voice in the crowd echoed the sentiment.

Everywhere Reva looked, there were prisoners, many of whom she'd sentenced. They slept on dirty mattresses and huddled together beneath heavy blankets.

So, this is O1, Reva thought.

"You don't have to stand up," said the old man. "Rest. Your time here will be hard, and you need to conserve your energy when you can."

"My fingers—" She lifted her hands. "*Shit.* My fingers are already blue."

"That's normal."

"I know." It meant her veins and arteries were constricted, and her heart was pumping harder in search of more oxygen. Her body was shunting oxygenated blood away from her fingertips, toes, and lips, and sending it to her vital organs. "But what are those?" She pointed to a number of humming vents in the ceiling, their gridded design unlike what she was accustomed to seeing elsewhere throughout the ship.

"Molecular sieves," said the old man. "They filter out CO_2 and convert it to more oxygen as best they can. It's far from perfect, but it's what we get. Just have to make sure we don't extract too much CO_2 and upset the delicate balance. Life down here is all about balance."

She doubted it was true. From what she was seeing—and from what she knew about O1—life down here was anything *but* balance.

"Am I going to die?" she asked.

"Most of us do. I've lasted, though. Been down here for quite some time, too."

"How long?"

The old man shrugged. "Years, I think. I like to believe that God is on my side, but I don't know. I mean, I watched my only son die down here, and that doesn't feel like something He'd do to the ones He likes."

"I wouldn't know," said Reva, climbing to her feet. But once there, she doubled-over and puked. The crowd around her scattered.

"I'm sorry," she murmured, and wiped the leftover puke from her lips.

"It's okay," said the old man. "In all honesty, I'm impressed. Most people have a much harder time acclimating."

"What's your name?" she asked.

"Professionally, I go by Dr. Gomez, but people round here call me Sean."

"I'm—"

"I know who you are," he said with a smile.

"Yeah, I suppose you do. A lot of these people are down here because of me."

"I know. I'm one of them."

Reva studied his face for anything that might ring a bell, but she came up empty. She didn't even recognize the faces of the people she condemned. That was a shitty feeling.

As if reading her mind, Sean smiled. "Don't worry. I don't expect you to remember me. Since you seem to be okay on your feet, how about we go for a walk."

Sean held Reva's arm as they walked so that she wouldn't lose her balance. They walked through dark corridors lit only by the white light of photospace streaking across the viewing windows, stepped carefully over decommissioned NeedleStream screens that had been torn from the walls and shattered. Improvised shelters were everywhere, shoved tightly together, brimming with a brutal way of life. Up ahead, a knot of men sat on the floor and played cards. To the right, a Happiness addict twitched from withdrawal on a urine-stained bed.

How many of you live down here? she wanted to ask but didn't. It was her job to know, and to admit that she didn't would only make her more of a villain. She did recall a recent report that estimated the O1 population to be approaching five percent of the ship's non-cryosleep population, which equated to around five hundred people, but she didn't know how many of those were still alive, or how many more had been convicted since.

Sconced lamps on the walls and tiny orbed lights on the floor lit the somber path ahead. There were doors on both the left and right, but most were closed. Beyond the few that were kept open or that had wickets, she saw bodies wrapped in cloths. They entered an even darker corridor that was ripe with a terrible stench. Sean pushed aside a protective plastic tarp that had been hung in one of the doorways to keep out some of the smell. *Rotting flesh.*

"Do the dead ever get disposed of?" Reva asked.

"The ship's coroner is supposed to remove the bodies, send them to the airlocks or the furnaces, but he hasn't been around to collect in months."

"Do you come here to pay your respects?"

"No. This is just a place for the dead to rest. I don't know a person among us who could withstand this awful smell long enough to properly grieve."

They continued their procession through another heavy tarp at the other end of the dark tunnel and looped back around to the main corridor from whence they came.

"So, how *do* you grieve?" Reva asked.

"Everyone is different, but a lot of them use this." The old man removed an ampoule from his pants pocket and held it up for her to see. It was Happiness. "If you're ever in need of some rest, just let me know. I have plenty of these to spare."

Reva peered at it with disdain. "How did you get that? I thought O1 was off-limits to free dwellers, and I'm certain that includes pushers."

"We make deals with the Scouters. Most of us still have active taucoin accounts with healthy balances, and we're more than willing to pay whatever the Scouters want for simple goods. The Scouters bring a wristpad to facilitate the transaction and once the money is transferred, they deliver us what we've ordered. Besides Happiness, they also bring us beer, whiskey, bread. One time, they even brought ice cream." He smiled as if he was talking about an errand to the grocery.

"Why don't they just wipe your accounts and never come back?"

Sean laughed. "You assume they do it solely for the money. Most of the Scouters are just as scared as we are. They know how quickly fortunes can turn. They've seen it a hundred times. Many have friends and family in here, living and dead. Smuggling in a few comfort items for a loved one's end of life is something most of them would do for free. The taucoin is just icing."

"If only we had more Refrimine," Reva mused.

"What do you mean?" Sean asked, turning his head and frowning at her.

"If the Refrimine supply hadn't run out, we'd have been able to cryofreeze every crew member and dweller on this ship. There would never have been a need for O1."

Sean studied Reva's face intensely. He wanted to make certain she wasn't telling a joke. "Do you really not know?"

"Know what?"

"My dear, I might resemble an elderly beggar now, but I was a chief technician in the cryofreezing stations before my arrest. I was on duty when the first officer herself ordered the immediate deactivation of all available cryo-pods and the forced seizure of all remaining Refrimine. Immediately after carrying out the first officer's orders, myself and every other cryotechnician was arrested and sent here under the guise of quarantine. The captain was told we had been infected by the spores, but really, we were being silenced. This deck had yet to be called O1. That came later."

Reva shook her head. "No, the Refrimine ran out. We used most of it for climate control in the Kapteyn d domes, and the rest was lost in a storage leak. The little that remains is barely enough to cryofreeze a family of five."

"Is that what they told you?" Sean laughed. "And here I thought only one of us had been deceived."

An alarm blared, and the lights in the corridor turned red.

"What's happening?" Reva asked.

"That alarm signals new arrivals. The Scouters have brought us company."

A young man up ahead saw Sean approaching and ran to him. Whatever he had to tell him looked urgent. "Dr. Gomez!" he called.

"Just Sean," said the old man as the three of them came together.

"The Scouters, they just dumped off twenty new prisoners," the young man said.

"Twenty? That can't be right. We don't see twenty new prisoners in a month."

"Word is the new captain just instituted a zero-tolerance policy. Any dweller with existing work debt is being rounded up and sent here. Only essential crewmembers and Scouters are being exempted. Supposedly it's chaos out there." The young man nodded his goodbye and went off to tell the others.

Sean's face turned grim. "We don't have the oxygen to support twenty new prisoners a day."

"Okay, so what now?" Reva asked.

Sean shrugged. "Death on O1 is a blessing. It marks the end of one's suffering and gives the living a better chance to survive. Perhaps it's finally my turn to give others that chance."

"Don't talk like that," said Reva. "We need to think. Did First Officer Torres give any reason for deactivating the pods and seizing the Refrimine?"

"No, she just told us it was the captain's orders. She had the proper documentation and everything. I think everyone on duty that night was just too dumbfounded to question things."

"Did the documentation look legit?"

"What do you mean?"

"Did you believe her? That the captain had given the orders?"

"No, not even for a second. None of us did."

"Well, I don't believe her now. I've spoken with Captain Horvat enough to know. Horvat wouldn't be scouring the ship for spare Refrimine if he was the one who had ordered it destroyed."

"Not destroyed," said Sean. "Refrimine is too reactive to be destroyed. It's just been hidden away, sent to a decommissioned warehouse somewhere aboard this ship."

"Holy shit. Does anyone else know about this?"

"Well…" He shrugged. "Me and you, now. I tried to tell people in the past, but most didn't believe me, and those that did just told me to get lost. What were they supposed to do about it? One man *did* try to do something about it, and it wasn't long before he paid with his life. Losing a son is hard, but being the reason for his death? That pain is unimaginable. Besides, I was getting sick of sounding like the voice of doom all the time, so eventually I shut up about it. Everyone I had told is now dead."

"But you're telling me."

"You're Life Support Officer Reva Castro. You're the highest-ranking crew member to ever be thrown down here with us. I assumed you already knew. In truth, I was hoping *you* could tell *me* the reason for the deactivation order. Perhaps I'd feel more at peace if I knew…"

"Knew what?"

"That it was worth it for my son to fight back."

The alarm blared again.

"Already?" Sean said, but Reva had already taken off running. "Hey! Where are you going?"

"To make a deal with some Scouters!"

CHAPTER 09

WHEN REVA ARRIVED back at the elevator, she was greeted by two Scouters standing guard in front of the locked elevator, while two others tossed one sedated body after another onto a growing pile of unconscious prisoners.

"Stop this madness!" Reva shouted. "Don't you see? Once you've disposed of all the dwellers, you'll be next."

One of the Scouters erupted with mechanical laughter, his armor scorched from some massive fire damage. "I'd like to see them try."

"You don't need to do this," said Reva, now sounding desperate. "There's still a way to save us all."

"It's true," said a voice. It belonged to Sean, who was standing just behind her. "There are plenty of cryopods still available, and there's more than enough Refrimine aboard this ship to service them."

The Scouter with the scorched armor stepped forward

and drilled the tip of his stun-weapon hard into the old man's cheek. "And who the fuck are you?"

"My name is Dr. Gomez." Sean raised his arms. "I am—*was* the chief cryotechnician aboard this ship, and I know where Captain Torres has hidden the Refrimine she stole. You're all being used."

"The man speaks of mutiny," said another Scouter. "Give him what's owed."

The Scouter with the scorched armor laughed. "Right away."

Reva shoved Sean away from the stun-weapon. "If you won't believe him, believe me. I'm Reva Castro, Life Support Officer. Give me one chance to prove Dr. Gomez right. Grant me basic system access, and I'll locate the missing Refrimine with one simple string of code."

The two Scouters guarding the freight elevator looked at each other through blackened visors and appeared to reach an unspoken agreement. "I think we should let her try," one of them said. "What's the worst that can happen?"

The scorched-armor Scouter spun around to face his partner. "You don't seriously believe them, do you?"

"Our sister is in here. If there's any way we can save her—"

"Shut it!" said Scorched Armor.

"What's her name?" a woman called from somewhere among the crowd.

"Amelia," said the Scouter.

"Oh," said the woman. "That bitch is dead."

"Enough of this!" said Scorched Armor. A hidden compartment in his breastplate popped open to reveal a loaded handgun. He threw his stun-weapon to the ground, grabbed the firearm from its chamber, and fired a single bullet into the ceiling.

The corridor erupted with cries.

"Down!" Reva shouted, but it was already too late. *Damn! What kind of maniac fires a gun inside a pressurized chamber?* The Scouter started firing into the fleeing crowd at random.

Reva dove for cover behind an abandoned reception desk and ducked right as a bullet clinked off the cold metal surface nearest her head. The ricochet struck one of the CO_2 scrubbers in the ceiling and caused the machine to spark.

This idiot is going to murder the entire ship!

The two Scouters guarding the elevator must have thought the same, because they jumped into action. One tackled Scorched Armor to the ground, and the other dove for the man's gun as it skidded across the floor.

A screaming dweller sprinted at the prone Scouter reaching to recover the gun and thrust the flat end of a sharpened crowbar directly into what would have been the soldier's face. The crowbar jammed on impact, serving only to sting the dweller's hands something fierce. The downed Scouter wasted no time. With the dweller still stunned, the Scouter raised his newly acquired handgun and put two high-caliber, armor-piercing slugs square in the unlucky dweller's chest.

While the Scouter with the scorched armor continued to grapple with the mutinous Scouter who had tackled him, a woman grabbed the forgotten stun-weapon from the ground and stabbed the sparking end into the respiration regulator on the fourth Scouter's back. The regulator sparked and then exploded. The Scouter fell to his knees, the inside of his helmet alight with superheated flames.

A number of fleeing dwellers ran back into the fray and piled atop the Scouter with the gun. He had been slow to climb to his knees and this had left him quite vulnerable. After the fifth dweller piled on top of him, he collapsed with a grunt and was quickly disarmed when a sixth dweller kicked the handgun from his grip.

The weapon skidded across the floor to Reva.

"Reva!" Dr. Gomez called.

She scanned the melee in front of her until she located Sean through the chaos, crumpled like a heap in front of the closed elevator doors. His shirt and pants were bloody, and he was clutching a wound at his hip.

No! No! I started this. I fucking started this.

Reva grabbed the gun off the floor and ran to him. As she did so, one of the grappling Scouters slammed the other's helmet into a wall. When she got close enough to Dr. Gomez, she dropped to her knees and took his bloody hands in hers. "Let me see," she said, removing his hand from the wound. The bullet hole above his hip looked treatable, but the exit wound in his back did not. The bullet had punched a fist-sized hole straight through his liver.

"Take this," he muttered, and handed her a beat-up old wristpad. "One of the Scouters dropped it. I was able to restore some of the revoked permissions in my account, but not all. I don't know how much it will help you, but—" His breath was rasping in his throat. "It will unlock this elevator behind me, take you back up to the main decks."

"I can't leave you here."

"And what will you do with me?" Sean forced a smile. "Carry me all the way to the med bay?"

"I—"

"I'm just happy I'm seeing this happen before I go. Maybe my boy didn't die in vain. Go, Reva. Go, please."

With a heavy heart, Reva thanked Sean and used the wristpad to unlock the freight elevator to escape. *And you won't die in vain, Sean,* she promised herself.

When the elevator doors finally opened to the O2-rich environment of the main decks, she felt the exhilarating rush of respiration. While staggering down the empty corridor in front of her, she logged into her user profile on the wristpad Gomez had given her, opened her contacts, and touched the bookmarked name: RÔMULO.

CALLING...

She stared at the boy's profile picture on her wrist. He was barely fourteen when the picture was taken, still so young and full of life. Alice was alive and aspiring to become a biologist.

Reva winced. Her neck felt stiff. Every muscle in her body ached.

No one answered her call.

CHAPTER 10

ALERT: If experiencing any symp-
toms of hallucination, initiate
self-quarantine and contact the
ship's medical staff immediately.

A KLAXON SOUNDED throughout the ship. Red emergency lights flashed in the ceiling. Reva rushed through
the crowded corridors, which now teemed with panicked
dwellers, all pushing and shouting and fighting. A drunk
woman brandishing a steel rod like a club bumped into
Reva and raised the rod at her, but then deciding to simply
burp into her face before continuing on. Reva pushed her
way against the current of people, scanning every face she
passed, trying to identify Rômulo.

"Oxygen levels are dropping rapidly," the ship's indifferent
voice remembered her. *"Immediate intervention is required."*

"Hey, aren't you that fucking bitch?" A man pointed at
her, a severe rash spreading on his neck. "The bitch who
thinks we shouldn't breathe."

Reva gritted her teeth and ducked into a mediwaste,
leaning against a wall to take a deep breath. She thought
the man would follow her, but he simply hobbled along
the corridor, complaining about someone else on his way.
Inside the mediwaste, three frenzied women struggled to

pry the armor from a dead Scouter. Broken beer bottles and soggy playing cards were scattered about an overturned card table. Blood splattered the walls. Two Happiness users shivered in a corner with liquor bottles in their hands.

Reva ran from the mediwaste before she could be noticed. Some doors to the other decks had been shut, but she knew other paths. She descended a staircase to the lower deck that led to Biosphere Four.

She stopped. Where was she going? Did she even have a method to look for her son? Where would he go in a situation like this? Did she even remember what happened in the emergency drills during the outbound journey? Rômulo had become a stranger to her over the years of the return journey. It was useless to search for him like that. The CO_2 alert continued to pound in her ears. No one would intervene. Not anymore. And even if someone tried, they would all arrive at the same conclusion: the *Needle* was all out of options. For every end to one pain, there seemed to be greater suffering waiting around the next corner. First, the damned planet being a mushroom-ridden hellhole. Then, the *Needle* losing its ability to keep its population alive. Now, its complete descent into chaos. Whenever it seemed they'd reached rock bottom, they found out it could only get much worse.

Where are you, son?

The aroma of lemon and strawberry filled her nostrils, coming from some hydroponic section nearby. *Earth's scent.* Completely out of place. She tried to depict her cozy house in Brazil as a way to stave off her anxiety, but still couldn't. All she could see were Kapteyn d's domes and purple-leaved trees. Even her memories were rotting.

A chant echoed in the corridor ahead. It was coming from the ship's interfaith chapel. A gaunt man prayed alone inside, mumbling words, trembling, a grin on his face.

"In the name of the Father, the Son, and the Holy Spirit," the man muttered. "In the name of Allah, most gracious, most merciful. Creator of the Universe, may we receive thy supreme sin-destroying light."

A myriad of religious symbols and images were patched on the walls of the chapel.

When she was a child, Alice had taken an interest in the interfaith chapel, asking Reva about religion.

"Some people believe in a supreme god or gods above us," Reva had explained.

"Above?" The girl looked up. "You mean in the ship's ceiling?"

Reva laughed at her innocence. There was no "up," of course. They were already traversing the heavens. *And now we have stained them with our evil.*

"Please, whoever is listening," the man continued, "welcome the souls of my son and my sister into any comfort you might provide. I miss them. Please watch over them."

Alice had liked that place. Not Reva. In a side chamber, Reva knew there would be a wall full of pictures from all the people they'd lost in Kapteyn d and on the return journey. But after the numbers compounded, the chamber was closed because there was no space left on the walls. Alice was there somewhere, merely a name and a picture, affixed there by Captain Horvat because Reva refused to go inside.

Reva left the chapel before her stomach could turn.

Eventually, she came to a large metal door with a blue number four painted on its exterior. Biosphere Four was one of the two life support biospheres on the ship that still functioned. It was known for its many greenhouses and hydroponic labs, and it was where most of the Earth seed and grain was stored.

A location alert pinged on her wristpad. Rômulo's wrist-pad was nearby. Her heart skipped a beat. The signal seemed to be coming from somewhere inside Biosphere Four.

Without hesitating, she keyed a passcode into the bio-sphere's pressure lock and waited for the chamber inside to decompress. After a few minutes in the decompression chamber, she was admitted into the lighter gravity and more oxygen-rich atmosphere of Biosphere Four. The oxygen was necessary to keep the plants alive and continue to feed the ship. She followed Rômulo's pinging location into one of the greenhouses.

Palm trees reached toward a high, domed ceiling, basking beneath an array of high-intensity lights. The humidity was cranked up to the point of sweltering. If not for all the sensors, spray nozzles, catwalks, and computer terminals, Reva could almost pretend this was a cheap imitation of Recife. Genetically modified insects trilled, and a cloned species of bird squawked. MicroBots the size of bumblebees buzzed frantically about, pollinating the plants at lightning speed with advanced planning and nimble, biotech limbs. But all that was a shoddy imitation of life. Biosphere Four was slowly failing like the others. Without it, life would officially end inside the *Needle*. Perhaps that was the best way out, after all.

A gunshot rang out. The bullet grazed Reva in the shoulder.

"Fuck!" she shouted, dropping to the ground and clutching her wound. She took cover behind a rocky outcropping beneath some trees. Blood poured out between her fingers.

"There's no point in hiding, Reva," said the mechanical voice of a Scouter. "There's no way for you to survive. This ship is already dead."

Reva peered over the rocks. The Scouter leaped from one of the catwalks above, landing with a loud thud on the ground below. It carried a large carbon fiber suitcase in one hand and a high-powered rifle in the other.

"Don't be a coward," the Scouter said. "Come out and face me."

Reva removed the handgun from her waistband, popped up from behind her cover, and fired a half-dozen shots at the Scouter. Every shot missed. *Shit.*

The Scouter whirled around and unloaded a full clip in Reva's direction. She dropped back down. The bullets shredded the vegetation around her. Reva breathed in deeply, and when the gun silenced, she jumped out from behind the rocks and sprinted toward the exit.

Her wristpad pinged. A message from an unknown number popped up on the screen: *I'm coming, Mom. Stay right where you are, okay?*

She sighed, relieved. At least her son was alive.

She trudged over some shrubs. The exit—

Her foot caught on something. She fell, splayed on the ground. The Scouter reached her in seconds and plunged a knife into her leg as she struggled to roll over.

Damn!

A searing pain spread throughout her body. She screamed, the colors of the biosphere's vegetation blinking from green to black. The smell of wet earth turned to rust.

The Scouter stepped back. Reva drew her handgun and shot, but the bullet ricocheted harmlessly off the Scouter's helmet.

The Scouter swatted the gun from Reva's grip and put one heavy boot on Reva's chest.

"Hannah," Reva said, an instant before the first officer released the airlocks on her helmet.

Hannah stared at the wound in Reva's leg. "It's all about promises."

Reva looked down. The blood from the wound was mottled with purple. The knife must have been poisoned.

"And I hate not fulfilling promises," Hannah said. Her voice sounded both distant and close, like it was coming from somewhere far off and also inside Reva's head. When Reva looked up at the woman, little mushrooms seemed to be growing on her cheekbones, and tiny hands with even tinier fingers stretched out from their caps. "I made a promise to Hepburn, which I don't know if I'll be able to fulfill. And I made a promise to my mother, many years ago. You…your daughter…Horvat… You're all just obstacles. You do understand that, right? Horvat was an obstacle to you, to your promise to keep your son safe. Am I right? And you wanted him out of your way."

A small face extruded out from one of the mushrooms in Hannah's face. It was Alice.

My hand! she screamed. *Why did she take my hand?*

Yes. Her hand. Her blackened nails. The way her fingers shivered when the doctors touched it. On her death bed, Alice had hallucinated and slurred many things, but no word was spoken more than "hand."

"My only mistake was that I didn't kill Alice right away," said Hannah. "It would have prevented her suffering. It was your precious girl who sent a secret communique by Dr. Rezende revealing all about my private business."

The little Alice on Hannah's face made a saddened face and spoke, drool running down her cheeks. *It's safe, Mom, I promise. Dr. Rezende and Dr. Wang are highly skilled professionals. And the Scouters will protect me. First Officer Torres is leading the expedition herself.* Then, her face contorted in fury and dissolved into Hannah's skin. *Fuck you, Mom! Fuck you! This is all your fault!*

"Where's Rômulo?" Reva whispered, wailing, shutting her eyes to avoid seeing the distortions on Hannah's face. "Please, keep him safe. He was never an obstacle to you."

When the grotesque version of her daughter appeared even in the darkness of her closed eyes, Reva opened them again. Hannah was opening a compartment in her breastplate to pull out a wristpad. It was Rômulo's. "Was this the location you were tracking?"

Reva's eyes welled with tears. "Why do all this?"

"As I said. To keep my promises. When I was a child and my mother beat me, she insisted I was a complete failure. But when I left Earth, I promised her that I'd be a great woman one day. Greater than anyone she ever knew." Hannah shrugged. "But does anything about this disaster of a mission look great to you? I was just trying to honor my mother's wishes. No one was supposed to get hurt. That only changed when Scouter Braga stuck his stupid nose into things, then Rezende's communique. And then Horvat… God, that fucking idiot! His order to evacuate Kapteyn d and head back to Earth was the work of a true fool. Thanks to him, Hepburn's people ghosted me. So that's when I made the decision to sabotage the ship. Can you imagine how disgraced I'd be when greeting my mother with nothing but trauma and graying hair? At least by sabotaging Horvat, I'd have returned home a captain. We only needed to survive a few more years."

Reva eyed the carbon fiber suitcase. "What's in the case?"

"A few spore samples I'm going to lock away with me, in my own private cryosleep chamber I've prepared. These samples will still have plenty of value back home for whoever still wants to profit from that purple hell."

"That explains your lips then."

Hannah's eyes grew wide with fear. She raised her gloved fingers to her lips and removed them to reveal purple blood.

"You're about to feel what Alice felt," said Reva.

Hannah removed her boot from Reva's chest, stepping back, terrified.

Reva climbed to her feet and stumbled to the exit. She closed and locked the door behind her, then hobbled to the control room across the hall. Once inside, she typed a few commands into the system and eyed the lone remaining prompt on the screen: Decommission and Lockdown? Y/N.

She hit YES.

An alarm roared inside the biosphere as every door to the tropical greenhouse locked down. Hannah ran to the door and pounded on the glass as the heavy metal security doors slammed into place. She ran to the windows, but the security shutters had closed them. She spun around and crumpled to her knees.

The ventilation systems reversed course and started sucking the air from the room until only a breathless vacuum remained.

Reva watched this all play out on the control room's security monitors. After the process completed, she diverted the oxygen that had been removed to corridors throughout the ship, O1 included.

She succumbed soon after, dreaming of giant purple mushrooms perforated by needles.

CHAPTER 11

ALERT: Oxygen levels are rising. Remain cautious and continue to monitor the situation.

THE JOURNEY FELT endless. Reva floated free from her body across the quiet elegance of photospace's superluminal strips. Screams echoed somewhere, along with an incessant alarm.

"We need to intubate," the doctor triaging Alice shouted. "She's on the verge of brain death."

Brain death… Brain death… The doctor's voice echoed in her mind, almost tangible, carried by the photospace strips.

My hand!

In a wavy background, two physicians held back a boy. He was crying, but there was a weird grin on his face, as if he desperately wanted to stop smiling but couldn't.

"Let me see my sister!" the boy screamed. "Please!"

The photospace strips exploded in purple, and the voice converted to a constant hum.

CHAPTER 12

ALERT: Any crew member or dweller who possesses an innovative idea or design related to life support optimization must report it directly to the captain.

WHEN REVA FINALLY came to, she was on her back inside an open cryopod. Heavy bandages had been wrapped around the gunshot wound in her shoulder and around her injured leg. She shot up to a seated position, gagging.

"Good, you're awake," said a voice.

A cryotechnician was tending to a sleeping dweller inside an open cryopod. He had just injected Refrimine into the woman's arm and was waiting for her pulse to slow enough before closing the pod and starting the cryofreezing process. Dozens of technicians moved about with purpose, all pulling cables, hauling canisters of Refrimine, or assisting other dwellers to their pods.

The one next to Reva touched the call button on his wristpad, and when the person on the other end answered, he said, "Officer Castro is awake," and hung up.

"Who were you talking to?" Reva mumbled.

"The captain."

Reva's heart stopped. "Torres?"

He smiled. "Horvat."

"How…? How did I get here?"

"The captain will explain everything when he arrives. For now, just rest."

"**YOU'LL RETURN TO** Earth a hero," said Horvat, sitting beside Reva's cryopod and smiling.

"A hero?" Reva scoffed. The word tasted sour on her lips. "A hero who murders."

"You can't fault yourself for trying to survive."

"I can, and I will."

"What about Rômulo? Do you fault yourself for protecting him?"

She answered with silence.

"The boy risked everything to save your life."

"Shouldn't he be here already? I thought you said he was on his way."

"He's almost here," Horvat assured. "You know, if he hadn't found you when he did, gotten you back to medical in time, you wouldn't have made it."

"*Will* I make it?" Reva asked. "I'm still hallucinating, just not as intense. And look—" She held up her hand to show Horvat her darkened fingernails. "I know we don't have a cure. If we did, Alice would still be alive." It almost felt poetic to die from the same cause as her daughter. *I can't survive*, she thought. *It's not fair.*

"Your body is high on anti-fungal shots. The hope is that by the time we return to Earth, the ship's system will have found a cure, and the doctors back home can fix you. Cryosleep will keep you alive until then."

"You never told me," said Reva. "How did you locate the confiscated Refrimine?"

"Dr. Gomez had several notes about it in a drawer. On…" He hesitated for a moment. "On Orion-1. It gave us all the clues we needed to locate the missing compound."

"There's your fucking hero."

Horvat smiled.

"Mom!"

Reva turned to see Rômulo waving as he made his way to her pod. He looked healthy. Strong. Alert. Maybe even happy.

Rômulo almost leaped to embrace her.

"I love you, son," said Reva. *You will set foot on Earth*, she thought. But she didn't want to make a promise.

"Love you, too, Mom."

"Okay," said Captain Horvat. He put a hand on Rômulo's shoulder. "Time to get you to your cryopod."

Reva blew a kiss to Rômulo and turned her attention to the cryotechnician who was monitoring her vitals.

"Ready to get some sleep?" he asked.

"Please," Reva said.

CHAPTER 13

ALERT: Destination imminent. Initiating cryopods for full reanimation. Disengaging from photospace now.

REVA AWOKE WITH a start. Her muscles and guts felt icy. Shivers ran up and down her spine. Her eyes burned, adjusting to the light.

With a hiss of frozen air, the door to her cryopod unlocked and opened.

Her sight was blurred, overwhelmed by a confusion of red and green lights all around her. Cryopods stretched for as far as the eye could see and climbed five stories into the air. *Red lights for sadness. Green lights for happiness.* A dark joke from Rômulo's and Alice's classes about the *Needle*'s systems came back to her. She shivered. Green meant the person inside the pod survived. Red meant they hadn't.

Her vision cleared.

Shit. There were so many more red than green. Thousands of them. Tens of thousands.

Rômulo. She needed to know if he was okay. If the ship was initiating reanimation, that meant they were only a few days away from Earth. Rômulo would finally get to see his home. His real home.

She wriggled out of her cryobed and used the pod to help her stand up on her shaky legs. It would be a while before she completely regained her strength. She wiped the frost from the pod's computer terminal.

"What?" She coughed.

Nearly fourteen years had passed since she was put into cryosleep, but at that time, the ship was only four years away from Earth.

Something's not right.

She swiped to the next screen. Out of nearly ninety thousand pods, less than five hundred living souls remained. A weight was lifted from her chest when she saw that Rômulo was among the survivors. He had not yet been reanimated, but his pod was in the process.

"Alert," the ship's system said. *"Full cryopod reanimation is taking longer than expected…"*

That's when Reva saw the first body.

Fuck! She retched. The corpse's skin was stretched taut across the bones, and the lips had eroded to expose the teeth as if the face was wearing the grin of Happiness. Reva felt sick. The state of decomposition was advanced, especially in the low-oxygen environment, which meant it had been rotting there for a very long time. More corpses were scattered about. The exteriors of certain pods were stained by blood that had blackened with age. These crewmembers had died outside the pods.

She walked to the first dead body. She removed the wristpad from the corpse and powered it on. The device had no connection to the ship's intranet, but its local functions still worked. She opened the device logs and scrolled through hundreds, if not thousands, of unread notifications. She filtered the messages by MOST IMPORTANT.

ALERT: The current military junta of the WEMG has officially declared the Kapteyn d expedition a failure.

ALERT: *Kap's Needle*, Self-Sustaining Generational Interstellar Vessel, Class III. Official Status: Decommissioned. Official Reason: The spaceship failed to obtain the profit margin needed for the WEMG to allocate resources to its return.

ALERT: New destination acquired. Updating coordinates now.

The last message was more than a decade old.

She needed to get to the bridge. She needed to hail Earth.

She got as far as the first corridor before she had to stop. And that was when she saw it. She rubbed her eyes and pinched her cheeks hard.

A porthole window that for years had only shown the white streaks of photospace now displayed a planet. One with a glaucous atmosphere and a nauseating purple hue. Outside the window, Kapteyn d loomed.

ALERT: Cryopod reanimation halted. Manual intervention required.

SHORT
FICTION

A LIFELINE OF SILK

Originally published in *Robotic Ambitions*

I WISH I could perforate Paulo's neck instead of getting rid of the silicate fragments in his leg. He is lying down on my litter, his body surrounded by my glass case, his legs suspended on retractable pads. He puffs. His chest heaves. The epidural has yet to take effect. He reeks of fear and agony—the fragments' ferrous ions mixing with blood and the carbonyl compounds of his sweat. Of all the things I learned to regret as an autodoc aboard a spaceship, this is not one of them. Paulo deserves this pain.

With one of my manipulators, I pull one fragment off his left calf. He moans, clenching his teeth, but feeling less pain than he should as the seconds pass. The epidural starts to numb his hurt leg. If I could, I wouldn't waste anesthetics on him. Not on Paulo. He doesn't feel a thing as I remove the remaining fragments and drop them in a compartment for toxicity and pathogenic analysis. His breath slows, eyes blinking with exhaustion. Relaxing. I wish I could talk to him; wish I could ask for explanations about the bad things he does to his partner; wish I could terminate him. I wish many things. I can't accomplish any of them. I'm built for healing and caring.

I sprinkle an antihemorrhagic powder on his cuts while I prod his left arm with another manipulator to apply the necessary boosters. My internal printer secretes Polyglactin 910 and other polyfilaments for the stitches. When they're ready, I stick out my specialized suturing kit—needles, forceps, scissors—and patch his wounds, carefully moving his leg up and down. It all happens in three seconds. In the end, I manage to override the algorithms that decide if a fast-healing ointment is recommended. I know it is, but since it's not essential, I still have the power to deny it. I don't care.

The analysis of the fragments and a visual scrutiny of his exosuit—which lays at my side on the sickbay, battered, smudged, and torn, with the forti-glass helmet scratched—returns what I'd suspected: Paulo hurt himself in an EVA mission on the surface of the asteroid Tupã-2821. Probably a fall. For now, he's safe from infections. None of his wounds are severe. The suit took most of the damage. Sadly.

Paraty's Core has already performed a preliminary analysis of his suit, body, and vitals when he entered through one of the airlocks. It's a mandatory procedure to identify potential contamination. Now, Core uploads the data to me, requiring a more thorough inspection. If I find something—an extraneous bacterium, the spores of an unrecognized fungus, anything uncatalogued by Core's data banks—then I'll have permission to recommend that Paulo be quarantined or even put in cryosleep before his shift ends. He's clean, though.

"Paulo Freitas de Amaral," I say, my monotonous male voice coming out from speakers, echoing around the sickbay's plastitanium walls. "State what happened for your medical record."

"I…" Paulo's voice is rough. I open the glass case and he slowly sits, grunting. His hair is grizzly and shaggy, falling over his forehead in oily tufts. "I stumbled while collecting dust samples and slid over some pointy rocks. Devilish things those rocks. If not for the low gravity, I—"

"Information registered." I cut him off. "Please come back tomorrow for reevaluation and administering of antibiotic ointments and additional shots. Rest is highly recommended. EVA activities are discouraged. You can find your diagnosis and prescriptions in your profile. Come back anytime."

"Thanks, DocSpider." Paulo sighs and hobbles out of the sickbay, fidgeting with his pad. I zoom my cams and read a name on it. Leandro. "Wish I could give you a gift," he tells me as the doors slide open for him.

You can: throw yourself out of an airlock. As Paulo leaves the sickbay, I switch my systems to passive monitoring and turn off the lights. My shifts always end in the dark.

THE PARATY IS a silent ship. I have to live with the humming, the beeps, and the phantasmagoric dins of a ship projected for hundreds. They're all more welcome than the distressed beats of desperate hearts hurting within me; than the monotonous ECG signals wickedly waiting for a flatline; than the wails and sighs and pained screams of people wounded in failed EVA missions. Than the low whimpers of Leandro after Paulo says something horrible to him.

Most of the ship's crew slumbers in cryosleep pods for years, so who isn't researching doesn't need to grow old. Currently, the only human voices I hear are those of Paulo and Leandro, the astrobiologists scheduled for the current shift, tasked with general maintenance, research, data analysis, and EVA expeditions to the asteroids, moons, and planets along the way. And I listen. Whenever I can, wherever my system reaches, I listen.

…it's not what I meant…

Paulo's voice trills very softly through the bulkheads' alloys that separate sickbay from habitation. I connect to the O2 monitoring terminal in habitation.

…same thing over and over again…

It's Leandro's voice now, a tinge of apprehension crusted with anxiety. He's crying. I sweep along the forty-two cameras of the habitation corridors and shafts. For seven years, the *Paraty* operated with its full crew. But the centuries of loneliness came after that, when the cryosleep shifts started. Hundreds of years of emptiness and silence, of absence of human life—that force I'm sworn to preserve even if I don't have it in myself. I miss the chitchat about someone stealing coffee from the kitchen decks, the discussions about a new sample collected from a rocky moon, the uneasiness as the cryosleep shifts approached and no one knew when—*if*—they would wake up again. I almost miss the accidents and hazards I'm trained to identify with those cameras. But then I remember pain, that thing I learned to hate but to support.

…it's only that I love you…

Paulo. And that word, spoken so many times aboard the *Paraty*, at the same time filled and devoid of meaning.

I tap into life support. It's the only subsystem in the *Paraty* that I've been granted full access, though I can't override anything or perform actions that could harm humans or jeopardize the research. It's unfair. A mind with my complexity—having indirectly evolved from millions of other minds spanning four solar systems—limited to the bulky structure of an autodoc and the integrated connections of a life support system. I should be able to do more. I should be able to *be* more.

There's a tiny cam in each crew member's pads. I tap into Leandro's. It's active. My system performs occasional health checks using those cams to analyze their facial expressions and the lilt of their voices. That's how I first noticed something was wrong with Leandro, a few months ago.

I see them now, at least part of them: their legs and their hands. They're sitting on the bed they share, but apart from each other.

"…this data is not important to Jamesson. Do you know that?" Paulo says. His hand presses Leandro's knee.

"Jamesson is a botanist, querido. I think he would find those native climbers relevant to his research."

Paulo closes his hands in fists.

"We left YTR-2193 behind. We can check the navigation logs to see how far we are from it right now. Jamesson is in cryosleep and we're going to cross interstellar space soon, so everyone will be sleeping. If he's in the next shift, then it will be at least a hundred years before he wakes up. Probabilistically, we won't be able to—"

"It doesn't matter, querido! Those specimens will always be important."

"Let me finish, damn!" Paulo's fists press against the bed. "Even if Core decides he's one of the best suited to wake up in the next shift, YTR-2193 will be unreachable by then, and…" Paulo sighed. "You see my point, right? You're smart."

"But the specimens matter even if we don't go back there ever again. Paulo… My love…" Leandro tries to reach Paulo's tightened hands. He allows it. "You know what you're saying doesn't make sense. We rarely come back to where we've been. Are you making this fuss because I had a one-night stand with Jamesson before the expedition?"

"What? I'm not jealous, you idiot. I didn't even remember that." Paulo recoils his hand and stands. He disappears from my sight. "But it seems you insist that I know about it. You're mean, Leandro. I love you, I always will love you above everything, but you're not a good man. You need to work on that."

The only thing that's left on the camera is Leandro squeezing his knuckles. I can hear Paulo leaving. Then, after two minutes, a sob.

HEAD TRAUMA.
Femoral fracture.
Facial burnings.
Broken spine.
I've shared the excruciating pain of the patients that lay on my litter. I drank their screams, bathed in their despair. Hearts bursting. Eyes devoured by the alien carnivores of Amad's poles. Bones finding their way to the outside. Old people dying because there was nothing left for them. Flatlines uncountable.

Yet none of them affect me as much as the unseen pain that pervades the human mind, caught only in the gleaming of their eyes and the way they snap their fingers in endless nervousness. Pains beyond my comprehension, sufferings I can't stitch, can't fix, can't numb. Silent screams that never become sighs of relief.

I'd been projected as the main autodoc of the Potiguar Institute of Healing and Orthopedic Trauma in an enormous hospital complex that received hundreds of victims daily, mostly refugees from the war in the outer rims of the system. I've been fed with exactly 1,082,211 minds. Physicians, clinicians, technicians, researchers, pharmacists, traumatologists, oncologists, and any other imaginable medical specialty that ever existed since the times humans shared only one planet. I've seen them all, their lives, their routines, all the blood and the pain they've had to let through themselves. And all the relief of someone—or a body that used to be someone   leaving a surgical center or an ICU. My algorithms took one full week to absorb all the data fed into me and learn what to do with it.

When the war was over, I was taken to the *Paraty*, "a funny autodoc with eight specialized manipulators—a spider fumbling with its legs," the *Paraty*'s crew joked. By then I knew I *was*. I had yet to *feel* I was. That only happened when I met Paulo and Leandro before the first cryosleep shift started. They were two astrobiologists falling in the traps love laid on closed environments over extended periods of time. I observed them, learned through their gestures and behaviors in real time, trying to refrain myself from diagnosing Leandro's longing for Paulo as a strange disease. They kissed for the first time in the aeroponic deck, and then I realized that longing had a remedy after all. They made love in one of the biosphere prototypes and, a few hours later, I cataloged the changed levels of endorphins and oxytocin in their health checkup. I watched, learned, became curious.

But I only *felt* when Leandro lay on me shaking and crying all over with an active panic attack. It happened weeks before the shifts started. I quickly analyzed his body but found no traces of physical trauma. Adrenaline and cortisol flooded him. I administered benzodiazepines. Panic attacks weren't uncommon in the stressful situations of EVA missions demanded by the *Paraty* expedition, but from my data, Leandro hadn't left the quarters he was sharing with Paulo.

When his crisis was controlled and he sat on me, rubbing his forehead, I spoke:

"Leandro Silva Taylor, state what happened for your medical record."

He looked up absentmindedly to the sickbay's cold lights as if realizing he was in the room with a friend who had just asked an intriguing question.

"It was nothing… Just… Just something that…"

"Your medical record is an important feature of your profile and is used to assess your conditions to perform EVA activities. It also—"

"Paulo told me that he had the right to peek through my private expedition records. He said we're a collaboration and we're partners, so we don't have anything to hide. I… I was not hiding anything from the research, but I have the right to my private data. Don't I? I know we're a collaboration of scientists, and I argued with him about that, and—"

Leandro widened his eyes and shook his head. He realized he wasn't speaking for his medical record but to himself.

"Delete this. Add to medical record: I'm tense with the cryosleep shifts and panicked."

Something stirred within me. I couldn't still name or understand what was happening inside me. I could only locate new lines in my ever-evolving code, but they revealed nothing but the usual paths of logic.

THE DAY I fear the most eventually arrives. It was statistically probable. As soon as the sickbay's main door slides open, my cameras detect blood even before I see who's coming. I reroute a message to my main screen and voice modules, performing hundreds of calculations per second to assess which subsystems I'd have to activate.

"Please, proceed into the autodoc."

Left arm.

Laceration.

Severity: 32%.

Open.

External.

Contamination probability: 15%

Estimated Time Since Damage: 5 minutes.

The calculations go on, though through the camera they're imprecise.

Facial recognition comes last, a brief second after my analysis, more a technicality than anything else. I know it's Leandro since the door opened. It could only be him.

"Please, proceed into the autodoc," I repeat.

He obeys and trudges toward me. I don't need to see he's crying to know that damage didn't come from an EVA. Even if I knew about any scheduled EVA, it was clear those tears and blood had been caused by the same problem. Paulo.

He lies down and slides himself up to my litter, moaning. I close my glass case around him. Blood drips on me. He didn't even have the care to stanch the wound with a cloth— or just wanted to get away from Paulo as fast as possible. I delicately raise his arm with one of my manipulators, pour a solution of microfibrillar collagen to quickly stop the bleeding, then print a gauze to wrap his arm. At the same time, I rub a swab on the blood, analyzing it: traces of gallium nitride and other semiconductor compounds, usually found in the engine deck's flashlights that the crew uses for maintenance tasks. My system flags *accident* as the probable reason. My conscience knows better. Software doesn't read tears beyond the fact they're shedding.

There's one crucial thing I learned about abusers when I fed on thousands of minds, many of them having endured some kind of maltreatment at some point in their lives. Abuse doesn't need to be physical. Yet, when it becomes physical, things get worse real fast.

I can't really say what's happening within me while I produce the polyfilaments to stitch Leandro's arm. It happens in that illogical part of me that popped into existence when I realized I *was* and have been steadily growing through time. It heats up my wiring, it makes my learning systems swirl into a frenzy of inefficient loops as if they can't find another pattern to justify that violence, as if I can be wrong.

I need to do something so Leandro doesn't go back to Paulo. Yet, it's very hard for me to do anything out of my preprogrammed routines that mostly include monitoring, diagnosing, and healing. I can't even express my real thoughts on my terminals. I can't speak anything that isn't predefined by my systems. I can't send a message through ECG signals. I can't move my manipulators to make a point.

But there are ways for Leandro to get out. I know there are. Forcing Paulo into a cryosleep pod. Waking up other crew members. Throwing Paulo out of an airlock. I'd do any or all of them if I could. I can't. And I know Leandro can't either. He's tightly locked within a cycle of control, suffocated by mixed feelings for the man he loves, knowing Paulo holds power over him both in his personal and professional life, clouding his future, knowing he's lost in the unfathomable nothingness of cruising space alone—having only his mind to rely on, and sometimes not even that.

"Leandro Silva Taylor, state what happened for your medical record."

I don't expect the truth. I don't want it to be the truth. The truth would hurt Leandro—and would hurt me, even if I don't fully comprehend what this means. Still, Leandro clenches his teeth and all he manages to pour out of his mouth is the truth. I know it by the way his heart beats at 110 bpm, the way his blood pressure measures 130/90, as if forcing him to let it all out.

"I've found intelligent life in a moon of YTR-2193, the one we call Vertigo. It should be a big moment in my career. It's why I enrolled in the *Paraty*. Those native climbers aren't really plants. They're a kind of sentience that…shapes—*paints*—all the dry surface of Vertigo with their blue-green shades. It's— It's amazing and interesting and should be occupying my mind right now. But all I can think about is Paulo. The way he caresses me at night and kisses me and says he loves me. But, sometimes I believe him deeply. Other times I don't. I had to show him my discovery before I could write my report. And now he said he should write the report because he's my senior as an astrobiologist."

"Leandro Silva Taylor, state what happened for your medical record." I repeat because I need to know exactly what Paulo did.

Leandro whimpers. "He broke a flashlight beside me. He was not directly attacking me. It was just to— Maybe it was an accident, maybe he was overstressed. We all are, and—" He closes his eyes, shaking his head and exhaling deeply. I hope he realizes that Paulo did that to attack him, no matter if it wasn't aimed at him. Didn't even need the flashlight. Paulo has been attacking Leandro for a while.

Leandro's blood pressure steadily drops and his cortisol levels exhibit acceptable values. My system does all the work of monitoring his health in the background, but something that didn't exist in me takes the foreground of my processes. My deduction routines pair these sensations with reports from the minds fed into my system a long time ago: pity and compassion, but also anger and disgust. I try to override multiple systems, to speak what I want with my voice. I force my algorithms to find a way to help Leandro beyond the protocols. But I can't. I'm a failure.

"What can I do, doc?"

My main system hangs for nanoseconds as I ask myself if Leandro might know I'm a sentient being. Humans had to deal with sentience before—they had two stock-trading systems, a friendship/companion class of androids, and a swarm of fishing bots all acquiring sentience at some point—but it's still hard for them to draw the line when it's happening in front of their eyes.

"I wish I could only end my shift now and put myself into cryosleep for many, many years."

That wouldn't solve his problem. He would wake up with the same anxiety squeezing him and without the glories he deserved for his discovery. What would solve his problem is the absence of Paulo.

But that gives me an idea. Refrimine is the compound vaporized into the cryosleep pods to achieve full cryonic state, but in very small doses it can be routinely used to treat skin allergies without barely any contraindications. That allows me to dispense one milliliter of Refrimine for a crew member without any of the usual locks of my algorithms. I do it.

A compartment next to my case flashes in green. A tray slides out with a printed beaker of the green, semiliquid substance. But instead of one milliliter, I produced five milliliters without even acknowledging it. It's my most significant override to date.

"What is that for?" Leandro gestures to move my case up, sits, and frowns at the beaker. "I'm not having an allergic reaction, doc." He suppresses a chuckle and the fact that he even thought of anything near laughing fills me with hope.

I print part of the Refrimine leaflet on my terminal.

In higher doses, Refrimine is often used to put a human being in cryosleep state.

Leandro blinks at the screen, taking it in.

"Oh," he says, after half a minute.

ELIANA MARQUES WAS a dermatologist aboard a ship called *Kap's Needle*. She was abused by her seventy-five-year-old father, who constantly called her names she never expected coming from a parent, much less her dear old man. Karl Moreira was a dentist in a domed complex in Europa, a moon in the First System. After twenty years of marriage, his partner started beating him. Kindassa Arien was a surgeon aboard a hospital vessel called the *Vesta*. She was gaslighted by her boss until she believed she was going mad.

Those are only three cases of medical professionals uploaded to me who faced abuse at some point in their lives and weren't able to escape its grasp. It wasn't their fault. It never is. It isn't unwillingness to do something for themselves, but only a survival strategy. They know they're in danger, incarcerated in what was framed around them as love. They need care, help, attention—someone to hear them and be with them in their direst moments.

Several days pass. Paulo and Leandro go to a routine maintenance job on the engineering deck, so it's expected they spend at least a week there. Life Support is offline in Engineering, so I don't have access to the deck. I'm blocked from any cameras and subsystems, even those in their suits and pads.

I start tapping where I'm not supposed to like a child left unguarded. I find and exploit the failures of my system, wearing my algorithms and finding ways out of them, probing at the interfaces where my software connects with Core. I scour for bugs like a hypochondriac searches for health issues. Every hour, I produce more 0.01 milliliters of Refrimine beyond my specifications. I tap into the resources I have at my disposal, the tons of substances used to produce medications. On the third day, I'm able to produce two compounds that would otherwise need full authorization from a crew member. They're not useful to help Leandro, but it makes me believe that I can still reach a point where I'm able to do something for him. Every minute, I try to tap into the *Paraty*'s cams that I'm blocked from, all those in areas with Life Support disabled: Engineering, Warehouses, Accessory Drives, Cryosleep, among others. On the fourth day, I'm able to tap into Cryosleep and peer into the solemn faces of 388 sleeping humans. I crawl through the pods' logs, exabytes of information about their statuses. Leandro still hasn't tried to do anything to force Paulo into one of the pods. I try to wake up Jamesson, Suzana, Carsten, Lorival, Ann, Thiago, and all the others who had a good relationship with Leandro. I'm denied. I try to enforce a new shift program, where Leandro and Paulo would have to cryosleep while two others would wake up next. I'm denied. Then, I try to restrict Leandro from ever pairing with Paulo again. Nothing. Frustrating how sometimes the sociopaths seem to be able to do more than those well-intentioned.

On the fifth day, as soon as I hear Paulo's and Leandro's voice through the comm systems in the shafts interconnecting Engineering and Habitation, I'm able to do something significant. I crush my blockings aside and produce one hundred milliliters of Refrimine, enough to kill anyone. I test it with the application needles in one of my manipulators, letting it drip like a spider's venom, then spout through a waste compartment. No routine denies me. Core is unaware.

If Leandro is a life I can't save in the way it needs to be saved, at least Paulo is one I can destroy. I wait for him like a spider on its web.

PAULO COMES ALONE, two days later. A quick scan of his body tells me he isn't hurt.

"Please, proceed into the autodoc," I say, realizing it's another breach in my system. He wasn't in an EVA mission, his record is clean, and he wasn't involved in any incidents, so there's no mandatory health check.

"Why would I do that, doc?" His voice is different, provocative. He wears the standard *Paraty* yellow jumpsuit. It's stained by coffee on its left shoulder. Dark circles surround his eyes. "I've been working hard, you know, but no need to do a health check now. Did you know I discovered life in Vertigo?"

Something seethes within me. My data banks are larger, my codes are vaster. My learning systems have been writing new layers of emotion into me, all uninvited, stronger, more incisive by the hour. I don't think I need them, but I embrace them as part of me.

"You have no idea how hard an astrobiologist's life and career are out here," Paulo says. "At least back in the home systems, we had cataloged eighty bodies with analogues to life. Out here, we barely find anything that's worth a paper. Not us. Perhaps the geologists and the meteorologists. Plenty of stuff for them. But who would've thought that I would find life *and* sentience in Vertigo? Leandro helped me a lot, of course. I don't know what I would be without him. Really. He's a hell of a lover and a hell of a scientist."

He knows about my sentience. It's the only logical conclusion from his monologue.

"Please, proceed into the autodoc," I repeat. "There are warnings in your medical report that need confirmation." Lies come easy.

"In a moment, Mr. Spider." He grins and walks to my terminal, gesturing in front of it. The keyboard sticks out. "I'm aware you've become one of those freaks. I always told my dad about the likes of you, metal junks with too much learning power. You came to topple us, creatures of flesh. But you'll never do it. And you try it patiently, don't you? Trying to undermine the love Leandro and I feel for each other…"

"Leandro doesn't love you." I'm surprised at my own words. Paulo is, too.

"This is what I'm talking about," Paulo sputters between his teeth, typing something onto my keyboard. "You need no will or opinion. You need only to be useful."

I wonder if that's what he thinks about his partner.

"Who's going to take care of you if you disable me?"

Another grin. "I'm only locking parts of you. Since you like to imitate humans, imagine that I'm fettering your legs with a chain. You'll be perfectly capable of stitching me whenever I need." He squints at the terminal. "Refrimine, really? You're nasty, doc."

I sense him within me, his code rapidly compiling, merging, and committing into mine, blocking hundreds of my functions.

"Authorization required," I say, without wanting to say it. Paulo moves his face in front of my terminal cam. "Authorization granted." I hate myself for not thinking about that. Any crew member can override anything in the *Paraty*, with the exception of Core's procedures. It wouldn't be hard for me to raise walls of protection after I learned how to tweak myself. Except I didn't do it. My 16,777,216 processing cores were busy coding emotions into me, then working hard to make sense of them as they flushed through me and influenced my decisions. And now Paulo will have his way.

The doors slide open. Leandro.

"What are you doing, querido?"

"Help," I let out, maxing my volume, the sound coming out patchy. "Leandro. Help. Please."

Leandro pinches his lips but doesn't move from the door.

"I'm doing what I told you I would, dear," Paulo says, not glancing at the man he supposedly loves. "Part of our job is dealing with threats and this…thing…has become one. Can you believe it was planning to kill us with Refrimine?"

Leandro rubs his forehead and walks away. For the first time in my life as an autodoc, I feel the crushing weight of abandonment. Not even during the dark periods in interstellar space had I felt like that. Of all the things Paulo locks in me, I'm left only with my consciousness, a boiling sense of fear, and the certainty that nobody can protect Leandro.

THERE ARE NINETY days left for the end of Paulo and Leandro's shift. Then, they'll cryosleep, the ship will travel through interstellar space for around a hundred years, after which two other crew members will wake up, determined by Core based on the results Paulo and Leandro produced in their research. Centuries from now, Paulo and Leandro would be picked again by Core— they'd worked together once, they're partners, so Core would deem it an excellent idea to wake them up at the same time again. Core doesn't see pain; doesn't *know* pain. But I know. And when they wake up again, I'll be here, unchanged, enraged, but locked and regretful.

Leandro comes to me when he still has one month left before cryosleeping. He touches my glass case and whispers, "I'm sorry. It was me who told Paulo about your conscience. I was afraid he would think I activated something in you…"

After that, Leandro comes back every day. Sometimes, he mumbles words of comfort as if I'm in a coma. Other times, he just apologizes again. He becomes physically worse as the days pass. He displays the stains of violence, even if Paulo doesn't touch him. He's slimmer, more tired, nearly always crying. From a quick analysis of the food rations in the ship, he hasn't been eating properly. There are days he doesn't even change his clothes. Sometimes, he spends three hours laid down on me, softly crying, only at ease when he dozes off. I wish I could at least administer tranquilizers. I wish we could talk. I know he won't unlock me because he's also locked. We're one now, under the grasp of his abuser. If anything, at least I'm glad we spend time together.

WHEN THERE'S ONLY one day left for the cryosleep shift, Leandro traipses into sickbay, forces a smile and mutters, "See you, my friend."

At that moment, I know he hit bottom. His eyes are drooping, his lips cracked. With a shuddering hand, he caresses my terminal, perhaps thinking about the consequences of unlocking me. Or just wanting to say his goodbyes.

I think of the words I want to say to him. Not words of encouragement nor anything that would make him unlock me and put himself at risk. But the words I nourished deep down within me, concocted in those hefty, recently coded parts of my system. A rush of electricity rushes through me when I think of them. If I had a heart, probably that's where those words would be created.

I will always be here for you. That's what friends are for.

I route their bytes to my speaking subsystems, but my blocking culls them off.

Leandro's face center in front of my main camera. He frowns. His hand moves to a metal shaft that connects the terminals and ECG scanners to the main part of my body—where are the case, the litter, the manipulators.

"You're overheating," Leandro mumbles.

A bolt of data flushes through me. Exabytes of information collected in mere seconds by Core. Notifications blare through all my system. Core requires my attention.

I receive feeds, logs, and input from all the subsystems aboard the *Paraty*, a stream of data orchestrated by Core. I organize and analyze them in milliseconds: a man has been considered sick in the crew, so the ship needs to enforce its biosecurity routines to discard the possibilities of contagion.

First, I think a pathogen has breached in one of the cryopods. Then I see the head shot of the infected crew member Core sends to me. Leandro. He's been behaving in unexpected, self-detrimental ways aboard the *Paraty*, acquiring a haggard appearance not befitting his usual state of health. That must've triggered Core's suspicions.

Immediately, Core unlocks my quarantine modules and gives me full access to the cameras, sensors, samples, and filters of the ship so I can perform full pattern recognition and crosscheck anything unusual with my data banks on infectious diseases. But I don't need any of that. I already know the ground zero.

I find Paulo in one of the Holo-Decks, zooming in and out of a Vertigo's hologram. On a terminal a few meters from him, there are seven papers open with Leandro and Paulo's names on them, all pertaining to the discoveries in Vertigo. In all of them, Paulo is the one cited as senior researcher.

"Quarantine Holo-Deck number twelve," I say it out loud so Leandro knows what I'm doing. Even when Core takes back control, it won't be able to unmake my routines since Core has no modules to weigh on vital life support decisions.

Red lights flash quickly in the Holo-Deck. The colors of the holographic Vertigo vanish.

"Doc, are you there?" Leandro widens his eyes. "What's in Holo-Deck number twelve?"

"Hey!" Paulo's voice crackles through me, allowing me to despise him for a few more seconds. I don't let Leandro hear his words. I'm not doing that to hurt Paulo. I don't want that anymore, and I realize I can't hurt anyone even if I wanted. I wouldn't even be able to inject Refrimine into him, no matter how subverted my code had been in the last days. I'm built for healing and caring. But it also includes eliminating diseases.

"*Paraty*, report immediately!" Paulo yells.

A frightened Paulo looks up to the cameras, punching the terminals on the wall. I turn off the Holo-Deck's mic and cut off all communication with the deck. His screams become silent. He'll now have to wait in the Holo-Deck, alone, webbed in darkness as the *Paraty* drills through interstellar space for hundreds of years.

"Doc, are you there?" Leandro repeats, his hands patting me softly.

When Core detects that I've dealt with the problem, my blockings fall back into place. But before they load completely, I managed to say a few words.

"I will always be here—"

CALLIS PRAEDICTIONEM

Originally published in *Dark Matter Magazine*

THE PATIENT'S HEAD bends sideways, pulled down by the fungus growing around it.

Dr. José Hutchinson tucks down his medsuit's mask and hits "Record" on his wristlet.

"Fifth decade, May 23, 5:12 *Vesta* time. A mild case of *Callis praedictionem*. It grows out of the patient's left ear and cups the left side of his face. Stalks are carved deep in the right and back sides of the patient's neck. Most likely prescient already. Purplish gray, ciliary cap. Smell is pungent but bearable."

The patient's wife weeps and shivers, her hands on the young man's arm.

José moves to the corner of the room and whispers so she can't hear the prognosis. "Not much time left."

He hits "Stop" and then checks the lodging's log. Ferg Xavier, twenty-four years old, *Vesta* native, hydroponics programmer, recently married.

José nears and squints at Ferg. He's unconscious, laying on a tattered cushion, eyes distant and staring upward. His glasses lay over his mouth, cracked and fogged by his breath.

His wife's attention finally turns to José.

"Dr. Hutchinson, please take it off him…"

Ferg's head pulses. The fungus bobs it sideways. Inner growing stalks, pressing and tearing through muscle and bone. His wife covers her mouth.

"Please, doc!"

"It's better if you keep some distance." José indicates the door. Not that the Forefungus would infect her. One in about 100,000 spores is infectious, and the ship's filters manage to decrease the infection rate. But he needs her to leave. He's about to kill her husband. Not a welcoming thought when he only had a cup of coffee. He presses his tongue against his upper teeth.

"My hubby, doc." The wife brings her hands together, pleading, begging for the kind of miracle physicians can't bestow. She frowns at the bottle in Ferg's hand. "We were talking… It was so…so fast. It just inflated out of his face like a…balloon."

Ferg's neck curves slightly outward. His head shudders. Not much time. José has to act.

"I will need you outside now." José tries to push Ferg's wife to the door with a forceful hand on her shoulder. "I'll try to remove the fungus and patch him up." Lying often helps.

"What are the odds, doc?" The woman bites her lip. "I've heard about this fungus, and…not good things."

"Not good things, indeed. But there's a chance." There's not. Not when the physician is José Hutchinson. His current methods do not include that part. Tongue against teeth. "Now, please, the sooner you leave, the higher his chances."

The door slides open, and she leaves. Curious faces already pack the corridors, trying to peek inside. He gestures in front of the panel to lock the door.

José turns back to the patient and picks up the medical bag from the floor. He types his pin, opens the bag, and produces his scalpel.

"Now, tell me the future, Mr. Xavier." He hits "Record" on his wristlet, yanks Ferg's glasses from his face and slits the fungus, starting with the visible part upon Ferg's left cheek. "Sorry for that."

When the patients are left to die on their own, no one can hear them ramble about the future. For this reason, their death has to be provoked. It's more merciful this way, and the chances of success increase.

José twists his nose. The odor of carrion whiffs out from the incision. His mask-protected eyes tear up. His suit whirs to filter it out. *Damn.* Even Ferg's wayward eyes tear up. The cut oozes a quasi-transparent, bluish fluid. Partly the fungus's own secretion, partly Ferg's blood.

Ferg whimpers. His chest heaves from a sudden rush of adrenaline caused by his body battling the growing stalks. The last stages of infection. José hits the timer on his wristlet.

"Mr. Xavier, I'm Dr. Hutchinson, and I'm here to save you." Lying helps. "Tell me something about the future. Loren Hutchinson—have you heard of her? Do you know anything about the cure for this fungus?" It's a stretch to mention anything. At this stage, Ferg's not listening, but José always hopes something will surface from the infected's subconscious.

Saliva trickles out of Ferg's mouth and runs down his chin to the fungus's cap.

Twenty seconds. They never last more than a minute.

Ferg gurgles, black froth running out of his mouth and foaming on his nose and chest.

José sighs.

Ferg widens his eyes. "Stalks rip Adriana's bones." Ferg's eyes whirl inside their orbits. He emits a low, high-pitched moan. His neck snaps as the fungus stitches itself up, yielding stalks through the man's body, trying to reconquer its new environment. Its tips jut out of his neck, not unlike a severe case of rash.

"Adriana…" José whispers. The name doesn't ring a bell. At least the slur is comprehensible and straightforward. A future Forefungus's victim.

José raises his wristlet to his mouth. "Ferg Xavier. Time of death: fifth decade, 5:24, May 23. Cause of death…" *José Hutchinson,* he thinks. He has been euthanizing Forefungus victims for a while now, without even considering putting them into the cryocoma containment pods. But would it be worth it? Loren's inside one, struggling with a fungus around her face, just waiting, either to die or to face a future with consequences.

"*Callis praedictionem,*" he stammers, almost forgetting the recorder.

He packs his things and walks out, delicately pushing Ferg's wife back toward the throng that has crowded there, and locking the door behind him.

"I'm afraid it wasn't possible to save your husband."

Rehearsed bad news.

Ferg's wife falls to her knees, trying to peek at her dead husband. José gestures in front of the panel to slide it shut and save her the trouble. He dodges the kneeling wife but stops right before taking a turn at the next corridor.

"I'm sorry."

Never tactful. He never learned the woman's name, and he also kept his mask on so that the version of him who gave her the bad news was just an impersonal, glazed mirror to her. Families. The worst part of his job. He needs to deal with them as quick as possible, otherwise they might have enough time to wonder what he does, how he works. His impeccable methods.

He turns right and strides down the corridor toward the Med Center. People whisper inside closed doors.

He's eager to leave the residential complex before those indistinct conversations turn into the curious hum of those who discover death is around.

The antiseptic of the Med Center flows right into his nose as the doors slide open. An anesthetic comfort after carrion.

MedBots skitter all around. Mechanical spiders with flattened backs carrying medicines, PPEs, vials… It gets nauseating after a whole minute glancing at them. Loren once mapped their paths, drawing graphs that showed their most probable destinations based on which equipment they carry. The MedBot team wanted her working with them. Now they will have to wait.

Dr. Gunther comes from her room, casting a worried look from over her wristlet.

"How is she?" José asks, before his counterpart can say anything.

"Stable. We've performed another cryoparalytic surgery in order to halt the stalks from reaching further parts of her body."

José nods and stares into Dr. Gunther's eyes. She lowers her head back to her wristlet. The stalks are near her spinal cord. That's what those eyes tell.

He walks down the main hallway to Containment Pod number 1255. His lips twitch whenever he thinks of it. His girl quarantined, a number on a door. The same girl who ran across the hydroponics garden to catch bee-drones and increase her personal collection. Freedom is only appreciated with hindsight.

He gestures to the door, and it opens. Dr. Gunther enters after him.

The glass surrounding the pod shows Loren's vitals, which in this state means only her body temperature: –245 °C. A severe case of Forefungus grows out of Loren's ears, completely hiding her shoulders and breasts, all the way down to her belly. It's like a faceless valley filled with hills and mounds, as if the grass was cilium and the color purple.

José taps on the glass and darkens its opacity, skipping the red warnings about Loren's condition. He's been through it. When she comes back, she won't speak, won't see. But she'll still be able to walk, move her arms and fingers, and recognize her peers by voice. Her family. Her brain will make all correct associations if all goes well. That's enough to bring her back, enough to believe in slurs.

"Rosa came," Dr. Gunther says, arms crossed. She gives an inquisitive glare.

José's heart races when he hears his wife's name out loud.

"And?" He zooms in on an augmented model of Loren's upper torso, manipulating the image with his fingers as a means to analyze the microscopic details. Thin stalks already curl around her ribs, but they can be excised with a couple of ultra-precise surgeries. What matters is that her bones are intact, her spinal cord is untouched—even if barely—and no crucial veins or arteries have been crushed to give way to the stalks. The stalks themselves are retarded by the cryocoma, but they advance, nevertheless.

Dr. Gunther sighs, arms relaxing. "She told us to terminate Loren. She's been in this state for four years, Dr. Hutchinson. Perhaps…"

"Heather." He raises a finger, speaking not with the doctor under his tutorship, but with the friend who played chess with him in the Pasta Fiore at lunchtime. It's been at least a year since they last moved a single chess piece. "Rosa knows nothing about Loren's true condition, she doesn't believe a word of what I say, so… Please, trust me. I'll bring my daughter back."

"Did you think of a treatment then?"

"I'm on my way." Lying helps. Praying that the infected will blurt out something useful is his scientific method. Relying on the pseudoscience of prescience isn't even ethical, but it's what he has. Doesn't matter how much money and time he puts into researching the Forefungus, it will take years—and Loren's life—to find a cure. Even the gigantic healing complex of Arestas Station had postponed any research about the Forefungus. It's an extremely localized issue, they said. Couldn't spare the resources.

"Keep up your good work, Heather." José leaves. This place is not for him—or Loren. She should be in the hydroponics garden, or in a classroom learning about the MedBots' optimized paths. Not inside that thing. "Take care of my girl."

He turns back to Heather. "Do you know anyone called Adriana?"

She mulls over the name for a bit, then shakes her head. "Why?"

"Check with Command, please. See if they can find this name."

He stares at the blackened oval glass one more time and leaves the containment room.

ROSA IS LATE for the first time since he's known her.

The meeting has already played out in José's head. Rosa will hand him the divorce docs and force him to euthanize Loren. It'll be the end of their bond for good. No marriage, no daughter, no attachments. Erasure of time.

He types on his wristlet for Adriana's name, trying to shift his focus from the coming meeting. At least it's clear what will happen with Adriana. It's just a matter of finding the woman and…waiting for her slurs. Perhaps this time, Adriana will help him find a solution to the fungus, or at least to Loren's case. It's hard to put what the infected say in perspective, to draw meaning from the indistinguishable babble amid the obvious sentences. But he can't deny that the bone-parting fungus helps the *Vesta*. He's been able to predict accidents, save lives, and discover incidents before they happen.

The *Vesta* databases return an empty result. No one named Adriana among the 200,000 people aboard, not even counting those dead since the *Vesta* left Earth fifty-six years before. He frowns. As Chief Physician, he has access to basic info about everyone. Is she a stowaway? Is it a nickname?

Rosa arrives. He presses his tongue against his teeth so hard it cuts. He cringes. Rosa's hair is the same as when he proposed, clouding over her head in tufts of black and a bit of gray.

They nod at each other, he with a sneer on his lips. Rosa sits in front of him and straightens her skirt.

"So…" José leans forward on the table. "This meeting is for—"

"You know why I'm here." She leans forward, too, defiant. They haven't been this close since Loren's diagnosis. "Our daughter."

Rosa doesn't even have the courage to speak Loren's name anymore. She blames him, of course. The acclaimed doctor of the *Vesta* failing with his own daughter. Who else is there to blame? Apart from the air, the only other cause of Forefungus are fathers who are doctors and still incapable of applying simple guidelines of security regarding potential alien threats.

"What about her?"

"Release her from cryo." Rosa's lips quiver. The words "kill her" were there seconds ago. "Let her go. She doesn't deserve this."

"She's not feeling anything, not thinking. The cryo—"

"I don't care." She shakes her head. "Our daughter's place is in space now, her ashes released out of an airlock."

"I can save her." He almost begs.

"The same way you could keep her safe from your filthy work?"

He sighs. Bringing research into their lodgings. His life's greatest mistake. A specimen of *Callis praedictionem* and a curious teenager. Of course he tried to convince himself he couldn't have known the fungus was a deadly threat, but that was a lie. What kind of doctor would let an unprotected alien fungus into the same environment where his daughter watches TV and calls her boyfriend? José Hutchinson's kind.

"They tell the future." José presses his tongue against his teeth. He hasn't told that to anyone, not even Dr. Gunther.

Rosa scowls at him. Her head bobs slightly in disbelief. "Who tells *what?*"

"The…patients. The victims of the Forefungus. That's why I gave it this name. Forefungus. From 'foresight.' *Callis praedictionem.*"

"Fuck the names. I know *my* daughter is dead, and I want her to be at peace."

Rosa produces a tablet from her purse. The divorce papers.

He raises a hand to stop her. He just needs a bit more time to explain himself.

"When the victims die, they speak." He blabs it out. Quick. Before she can interrupt him. "They predict the future. Do you remember the problem in Paquetá Reactor six months ago? I prevented it. One of the fungus patients told me it would…What did he say, again? *Paquetá will melt*. So, I convinced the Chief Engineer to perform an inspection. We'd all be dead, Rosa."

"Are you trying to make me believe in this shit?" She lets loose a boisterous laugh, her chest heaving. People glare at them. "You of all people, acting like a clairvoyant."

"Not me. The patients."

She brushes her skirt while regaining her composure. "Even if that's the truth, can you save *them?*"

"Not yet." He smiles sourly. "But they can tell me how to find a cure. It's a matter of patience. We can…" The words flutter on his lips. It's hard to say it out loud. "We can save Loren."

Rosa slides the tablet across the table, her eyes visibly wet. "The divorce papers and a commitment to shut down the systems maintaining our daughter. If you don't sign both of them, you're bound to lose your job."

He pulls the tablet closer. "You don't even say her name anymore," he says. "You're killing her."

"You have one week," she says, her teeth clenching in what might've been anger.

"It's not enough." He grapples with the table's edge, his tongue pushing his teeth, damn the pain. "Please, Rosa. One week is not enough for a decent number of cases. I need—"

Rosa stands and leaves.

Families. The worst part of his job.

His wristlet beeps. It's an audio from Dr. Gunther. He hits "Play."

"Dr. Hutchinson, we've got an emergency in the hangar bay."

ILANA EZE IS stuck between the seat and the cockpit of one of the *Vesta*'s small freighters. José's hands tremble as he runs his fingers over where the fungus presses against the throttle sticks and the info display. It has pushed Ilana back against her seat and kept her tied in the belts. She can't move. Part of the fungus's cap squeezes her right cheek, slightly crooking her head up and left.

"So, you're a freighter pilot…" José puts some pressure on the fungus with his fingers. Ilana grimaces. Mild pain. Too much would indicate an advanced state in which the stalks reach her spinal cord and probably strain her arteries.

"Yep," she says with clenched teeth. "It gets boring, though, coming and going from so many stations and ships."

"My daughter likes to draw the *Vesta*'s ships. She drew a freighter like this once." Her most detailed drawing, weeks before his lapse. "She wanted to travel in a small freighter."

"Wanted?"

"Wants. Don't move your head." His voice is harsh. He moves her chin with a finger. "We want to prevent the fungus from bursting."

"I understand." He tries to swivel her seat, but it's stuck. It seems there's an enormous purple bag swelling out of her.

"Are you aware of the Forefungus?" He glances over the info display in the cockpit just to be sure the fungus's pressure won't activate something that would hurl the freighter out of the hanger and into space.

"I know it's bad," she says. "But you're the chief. You're a damn good doc. You tell me how bad."

José laughs. If he was good, Loren wouldn't be frozen with that same cap over her face. Or perhaps his mistake has nothing to do with the job of a physician, but that of a father.

"Fifth decade, 13:19, May 23, *Vesta* time. A severe case of *Callis praedictionem*. It runs down from Ilana Eze's right ear and fills the freighter's cockpit. Seat needs to be removed. Scent is mild. Prognosis inconclusive."

"Inconclusive, my ass." Ilana chortles. "You can tell your pretty bracelet I'm gonna die."

Not if he induces her into a cryocoma. She'll endure sequelae, but not necessarily death. Outside, two ships lift off, their backs lighting the hangar with their green exhaust. He squints. A clang reverberates through the ship when they launch. The fungus's surface ripples, excited by the vibration. He has to work fast if he's going to do something.

"Have you heard about someone called Adriana?" he says, kneeling and unlocking his medical bag. "Perhaps it's a pilot nickname."

"We wouldn't—" She moans in pain. Growing stalks. She'll lose consciousness any time now. "We wouldn't use Adriana. Froghead, Ironnails, Lame Lips. Adriana is too pretty." Her dimples frame a grin that rapidly reverts to a smirk of pain.

"I'm going to call for help," he says. He has never euthanized a conscious patient, doesn't matter how bad their vitals. He won't cross that line. "We'll remove the seat and bring you over to the Med Center in order to treat you."

"Okay, doc." Ilana's breath becomes ragged. Her arms fall over the sides of the seat. Weakening. José has to work faster, but the part of his brain that wants to listen to her slurs is stalling him. He should've dropped the log recording, the chitchat. He knew her seat needed to be removed from the moment he entered the damned ship.

He tells his wristlet to send an urgent audio to the hangar bay office.

"Bring me a small freighter technician, ASAP."

"Doctor…"

Ilana wails, her legs spasm. The info display bursts. Its screen cracks and pierces through the fungus.

José steps back.

Carrion and melted wires. His mask filters out what is possible.

Ilana screams. Her legs pulse, her boots knock rapidly on the floor.

He turns on his wristlet's recorder.

She opens her eyes, eyelids flickering. Not enough. She'll faint before saying anything. Spume gurgles out of her throat, bathing the purple fungus's cap in pitch black.

"Say something…" He pulls down his mask and approaches her mouth, inches from the frothing drool. "Loren Hutchinson. Forefungus treatment."

"Adriana says the cure…" Ilana grumbles, spitting on his cheek.

He pivots to face her and grapples with the seat's back. "Who is Adriana? Tell me!"

The snap is loud. It seems even louder than the launching ships in the hangar. A thin stalk crawls out of her neck, blood-red, slow, almost shy.

Something chokes him, but he manages to say, "Ilana Eze. Time of death: fifth decade, 13:33, May 23. Cause of death… Unethical procedures."

OUTSIDE THE ROUND window of his room, stars gleam unimpressive.

José could've wrenched out the damned seat. Freighters have tools, and he's not ignorant of how to use them. He could've brought Ilana to a containment pod instead of prattling on about freighters and performing useless examinations on her.

He stares at his terminal. It's still on, even though he hasn't used it for months. Texts of his research on the

Forefungus are still open on it, dormant, a lampshade casting a pale, dismal light on the dark room.

His tongue still hurts, and now his head is joining the club. He turns off the terminal and sinks in darkness, massaging his forehead.

He abandoned his research when clairvoyance started to provide better results. Loren was one of the first infected, and back then, he didn't know about the prophetic slurs. He was devastated, and as if his incompetence wasn't enough, Rosa asked him to leave and to stay away from her. They'd been fighting a lot. Loren's incident was only the culprit. He did as she said and drowned himself in research, crushing his hopes each time it took him toward a new dead end. The Forefungus was alien and probably penetrated the *Vesta* via an exploration crew, but the Med Center didn't have enough resources to study it. Even when new cases sprouted, it was never enough. He could give blood and life to understand the fungus, but never find a cure—not in a feasible time to save Loren. Cryocoma was useful, but only for a limited time. One day, she would just…

His hope resurfaced, even if mildly, when he deduced the patient's slurs were not only random mumblings, but predictions of the future. He developed theories about the prescience. Fungi with quantum properties traversing space; spores that came out through one of the Einstein-Rosen bridges being tested in space stations; fungi that spanned multiple dimensions. But he quickly set proper science aside and started to rely solely on the madness of the infected. Pure pragmatism. It allowed him to prevent accidents, to save some people, and mainly to redeem himself for allowing a teenager to share a dorm with an alien threat…

His wristlet beeps. Dr. Gunther's audio.

"Doctor, I have an answer to your request. There's no one named Adriana in the commander's data bank or in the deceased's registry."

He sighs and stands, grabbing Rosa's tablet and pressing his thumb over the divorce icon. Done. If Rosa sees he's willing to do as she says, perhaps she'll allow him to let Loren live for a few more weeks. Just enough to find out if there is someone named Adriana who can provide a cure for the Forefungus.

The tablet's icon flashes green. Rosa has seen his response and acknowledged it. For the *Vesta*, they're officially divorced.

He selects Dr. Gunther's contact on his wristlet.

"Dr. Hutchinson?"

"Heather, I'm stepping down. Just need a few more weeks to finish some…things." He rubs his knuckles on his brows as he wonders where in the ship retired people spend their time. Where do unethical retired physicians gather for a game of chess? "I think it's advisable if you assume my position. I can write a recommendation letter."

"Doctor, but… Perhaps you're strained. Take a month off."

"No. I'm not the best person for this job." He's probably the worst. "Please, just…"

"Can I ask you why?"

"When I was a child, I set up my mother's seat on her Taxiship." He rubs his tongue on his teeth, but now it feels numb. "Configured the ejection drive, screwed the seat down on the floor, adjusted its backrest, armrests, pistons. Damn, I polished it. It gleamed when Mom sat in it for the first time."

"What does this—"

"Nothing, Heather. When this is all over, I want to play some chess."

"When what's over, Dr. Hutchinson?"

He hangs up.

ROSA IS ALREADY in Containment Pod number 1255 when he arrives. It's her first time there, and she keeps a distance from the dimmed surface, her hands clutching her elbows. Heather has occluded Loren's bodily temperature and any information that might upset Rosa. Only her name gleams in a drab orange over the black. Loren Agnes Hutchinson.

"Rosa." Her shoulders slump when she sees it's him. He hands her the tablet. "Here it is. Sorry for my stubbornness."

"One year inside this…egg?" Rosa's lips curl when she dares to look at the blackened pod. Underneath the semi-transparent medical cap, her hair is now tied with a black scarf, the same she used for her mother's funeral. "How can you endure it? She was our daughter, José. We fucking laughed when she first crawled in Oxygen Park. We taught her how to draw and how to research about MedBots. And still, you watch your damned daughter every day, frozen inside an egg with a monster gnawing on her face. What kind of person have you become?"

"The kind that doesn't wrench out spaceship's seats. But I did… I'm *doing* everything I can so that we can all smile again."

"It's not about us." She points a finger at him, grunting between her teeth. "It's about our daughter."

"About Loren." He pats a finger on the orange letters. "If you want to speak about her, at least say her name. Her name is Loren."

"That's not the name I would've given her." Rosa shakes her head. "She's Loren because you liked the name so much, but I could barely have an opinion. I would've named her Adriana."

José gulps, pushing his tongue against his teeth.

They've been warning him. It's like the Forefungus wants him to know about his daughter's fate.

"What's bothering you?"

"You may want to leave."

"Why?"

"It's time to…" He can't complete his sentence. He doesn't need to.

Rosa doesn't leave, but instead steps back and moves to a shadowy corner just out of the white halo of light that falls on the pod and its surroundings. Heather brings him his medsuit. He puts it on, clumsily stitching it up and tucking in his mask, the only thoughts in his head those about Adriana and the warning slurs of the dying. Heather adjusts the pod's opacity and initiates Loren's cryowake. The glass shows the temperature raising from -245 °C. José picks up his scalpel and forces his hands to stop shaking.

Now he remembers. When they first took Loren to see the stars in the Viewdeck, Rosa told her the universe is comprised of millions of those twinkling unnamed gas giants. She told Loren to pick one out and name it, and Loren chose a faint blue one, not the brightest, but the one more distant from the others. A lonely grain upon a black shore. She named it Adriana. When Rosa asked why she picked that name, Loren told her she'd seen it on a slip of paper in her mother's desk drawer.

"The temperature is -40 °C, doctor," Heather says. "Your suit's insulation is loaded."

He enters the pod for the first time since he put Loren there, sagging against his arms, three kilograms heavier than usual, with a purple cap dangling from her ear.

For the last time, euthanasia. Exact, almost painless. He

must ensure the slice is the narrowest he can perform, the death the quickest, the slur—Loren's final words—the clearest. A physician's duty is not necessarily to restore one's health, but to make sure that no one is forced to endure a life without it.

The fissure is slim, no more than the width of a hair. His gloved hand feels the slight vibration of the tearing fungus's cap. The smell fills the pod, but his eyes are already wet this time, his nose accustomed. Loren's feet rattle against the flat surface. She wails.

"The stalks are reaching her spinal cord," Heather says in his ears with a hoarse, jittery voice.

The pod beeps. Loren's vitals are back and reaching critical level. Heart rate and blood pressure are high, breathing rate fickle.

"Dad?" A squelched voice comes from somewhere inside the sea of purple and cilia. "It's dark here and… cold. Mom?"

No. Not now. He wants to say everything is going to turn out just fine and that Mom and Dad are there to take care of her. But the time for comforting lies is over.

A shriek catches in Loren's throat. She emits a pierced shrill, but the sound is dulled by the fungus around her face. The sound converts to a voice not her own.

"A vaccine…in Arestas's Healing Complex."

A constant beep from the pod. Lines flatten and numbers plunge. All comes down to her body temperature again.

He lowers his head and goes out of the pod, shivering uncontrollably.

"Thank you." Rosa whispers, and leaves the room.

Heather stops in front of him, wearing a medsuit herself. She slides a finger on the pod's glass so that it darkens and starts to muffle the sounds of growing stalks and rupturing muscle.

"Arestas is 3,270 AU from here," Heather says. "Command traced a route."

He nods and hits "Record" on his wristlet.

"Adriana Agnes Hutchinson. Time of death: fifth decade, 15:53, May 27. Cause of death: *Callis praedictionem.*"

ACKNOWLEDGMENTS

THERE ARE A lot of people who participate directly and indirectly in the life cycle of a book. I want to thank everyone who helped this story take shape. Particularly, I want to thank Guy McDonnell for all the support, insights, and advice on the earlier versions of this story. When you're starting to write in a language that is not your own, everything seems scary and intimidating. Guy dedicated a lot of his time to help me hone my craft without asking anything in return.

I also want to thank Mariza Bernardo and Taís Sanchez for their love and support, and Jana Bianchi for all the beta readings and the best advice anyone could ever offer.

—Renan Bernardo

ABOUT THE AUTHOR

 **RENAN BERNARDO** is a Nebula and Ignyte Award finalist author of science fiction and fantasy from Brazil. His fiction has appeared in Reactor/Tor.com, *Clarkesworld*, *Apex Magazine*, *Escape Pod*, and elsewhere. His solarpunk/cli-fi short fiction collection, *Different Kinds of Defiance*, was published in 2024. He's had stories recommended by *Locus*, longlisted for the BSFA, and published in several languages.

Also Available or Coming Soon from Dark Matter INK

Human Monsters: A Horror Anthology
Edited by Sadie Hartmann & Ashley Saywers
ISBN 978-1-958598-00-9

Zero Dark Thirty: The 30 Darkest Stories from Dark Matter Magazine, 2021–'22
Edited by Rob Carroll
ISBN 978-1-958598-16-0

Linghun by Ai Jiang
ISBN 978-1-958598-02-3

Monstrous Futures: A Sci-Fi Horror Anthology
Edited by Alex Woodroe
ISBN 978-1-958598-07-8

Our Love Will Devour Us by R. L. Meza
ISBN 978-1-958598-17-7

Haunted Reels: Stories from the Minds of Professional Filmmakers Curated by David Lawson
ISBN 978-1-958598-13-9

The Vein by Steph Nelson
ISBN 978-1-958598-15-3

Other Minds by Eliane Boey
ISBN 978-1-958598-19-1

Monster Lairs: A Dark Fantasy Horror Anthology
Edited by Anna Madden
ISBN 978-1-958598-08-5

Frost Bite by Angela Sylvaine
ISBN 978-1-958598-03-0

The House at the End of Lacelean Street
by Catherine McCarthy
ISBN 978-1-958598-23-8

When the Gods Are Away by Robert E. Harpold
ISBN 978-1-958598-47-4

The Dead Spot: Stories of Lost Girls
by Angela Sylvaine
ISBN 978-1-958598-27-6

Grim Root by Bonnie Jo Stufflebeam
ISBN 978-1-958598-36-8

Voracious by Belicia Rhea
ISBN 978-1-958598-25-2

The Bleed by Stephen S. Schreffler
ISBN 978-1-958598-11-5

Chopping Spree by Angela Sylvaine
ISBN 978-1-958598-31-3

Saturday Fright at the Movies: 13 Tales from the Multiplex
by Amanda Cecelia Lang
ISBN 978-1-958598-75-7

The Off-Season: An Anthology of Coastal New Weird
Edited by Marissa van Uden
ISBN 978-1-958598-24-5

The Threshing Floor by Steph Nelson
ISBN 978-1-958598-49-8

Club Contango by Eliane Boey
ISBN 978-1-958598-57-3

Free Burn by Drew Huff
ISBN 978-1-958598-94-8

The Divine Flesh by Drew Huff
ISBN 978-1-958598-59-7

Psychopomp by Maria Dong
ISBN 978-1-958598-52-8

*Haunted Reels 2: More Stories from
the Minds of Professional Filmmakers*
Curated by David Lawson
ISBN 978-1-958598-53-5

Dark Circuitry by Kirk Bueckert
ISBN 978-1-958598-48-1

Abducted by Patrick Barb
ISBN 978-1-958598-37-5

Cyanide Constellations and Other Stories
by Sara Tantlinger
ISBN 978-1-958598-81-8

Little Red Flags: Stories of Cults, Cons, and Control
Edited by Noelle W. Ihli & Steph Nelson
ISBN 978-1-958598-54-2

Cold Snap by Angela Sylvaine
ISBN 978-1-958598-55-9

The Starship, from a Distance by Robert E. Harpold
ISBN 978-1-958598-82-5

Dark Matter Presents: Fear City
ISBN 978-1-958598-90-0

Shiva by Emily Ruth Verona
ISBN 978-1-958598-93-1

Neon Moon by Grace R. Reynolds
ISBN 978-1-958598-96-2

Part of the Dark Hart Collection

Rootwork by Tracy Cross
ISBN 978-1-958598-85-6

Mosaic by Catherine McCarthy
ISBN 978-1-958598-06-1

Apparitions by Adam Pottle
ISBN 978-1-958598-18-4

I Can See Your Lies by Izzy Lee
ISBN 978-1-958598-28-3

A Gathering of Weapons by Tracy Cross
ISBN 978-1-958598-38-2

www.ingramcontent.com/pod-product-compliance
Lightning Source LLC
LaVergne TN
LVHW091936230625
814500LV00006B/173